BONDED
BY
DESTINY

COMPANION NOVEL TO
THE FAE KING DUOLOGY

TM GOODKEY

Credit

Cover Designer: Emcat Designs
Editor: Dead Trees and Ink

Contents

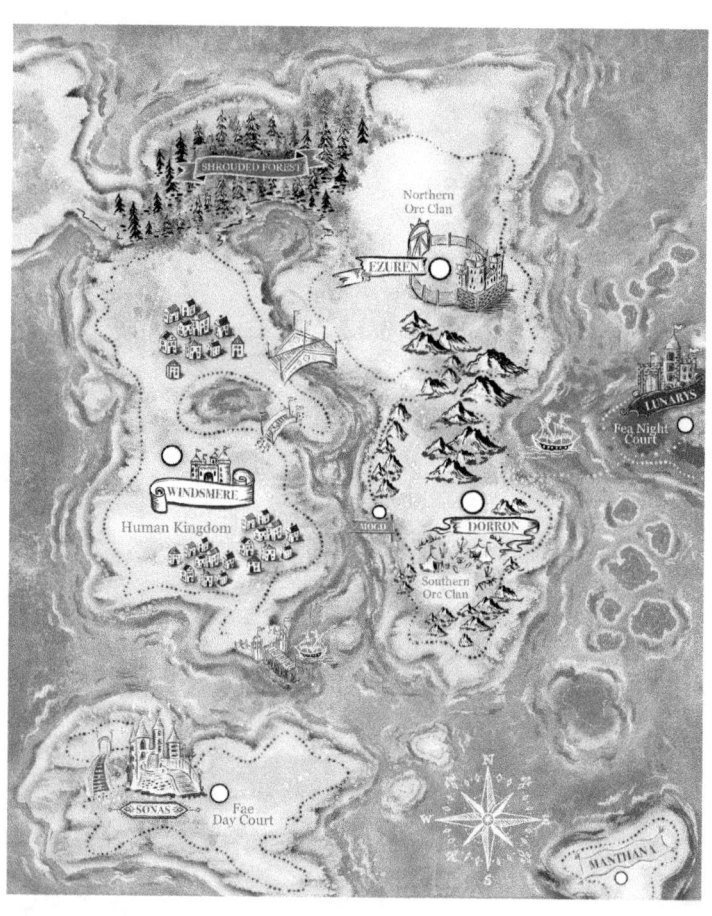

This is dedicated to all the people who liked my first books so much they asked for this story.
Wouldn't be writing without that encouragement.
Thank you.

Author Note

W elcome back! This is the third book in the Fae King Series! How crazy is that!?

This book is about Garrick. We left off with him chasing after Alette, the Human princess, after he finally decided not to be an idiot and do something about the bond!

The beginning of the story takes place a couple weeks before Alette leaves to return to the Human Kingdom, Windsmere.

Buckle up and enjoy the ride, this story really became more than just Garrick chasing after Alette, it became a story of two people overcoming fear and duty.

TM

PLEASE NOTE!

I am Canadian and write in Canadian English, if you think it is spelt wrong it may just be spelt in Canadian English.

Chapter 1

Garrick

Emilia said if I injured another Fae noble she would let them stick me in jail... though in my defence, the last time wasn't entirely my fault. And this time definitely won't be my fault either—not with how Lord Astralius is currently fawning over Alette.

"It would be an honour to escort you to the Night of the Golden Trail. Your first time, if I'm correct?" His voice grates on me like metal on glass. The gold jacket he's wearing probably costs more than I make in a year, which just adds to his pompous presence.

When he reaches out to tuck a strand of Alette's hair behind her ear, the darkness that's been growing inside me surges. The sword I'm sharpening suddenly feels like it would make a perfect projectile for his pretty little head.

"Oh, well, that's awfully kind of you but um... I'm not sure I would be good company." Alette's sweet voice momentarily calms the inferno raging through my blood, but watching him hover over her like some overdressed vulture has my hands shaking with barely contained fury.

I push the whetstone harder against the blade, desperately focusing on the familiar spray of sparks. But even the screech of metal on metal can't drown out that pretentious Fae's voice.

"Nonsense! You are a guest of the king and queen! It would be horribly rude if one of the noble houses didn't escort you. To ensure your safety, of course. Purely a polite gesture."

I watch as Alette steps back, but Astralius follows, claiming her space like he owns every inch of ground he stands on. The burning sensation that's become my constant companion since trying to ignore the bond travels up my arms. The small sparks from the whetstone turn to flames of pure rage.

"Well, I suppose if it is merely polite." The resignation in her voice makes something aggressive rise in my chest. My muscles coil with unrestrained anger, and the whetstone slips. The blade's edge opens my skin from thumb to wrist.

"DAK!" I curse, dropping both blade and stone. Dark red blood immediately wells up from my green skin while I reach for a rag. This is exactly why I've been avoiding her. One month of carefully planned routes through the palace, of hiding in the forge, all undone because I can't focus with her near. The soul bond pulses angrily, punishment for my resistance these past couple of weeks.

"Are you alright?" Her voice startles me from my thoughts. The tug in my chest becomes incessant, her presence a few feet away pulling at the deepest part of my soul. Every instinct screams to embrace her, to claim what the goddess has given to me.

My lips press against each other, one half out of relief, the other to retain the little control I have left. "Fine."

I need her to leave. I hate acting so cold towards her, but this is the only way to protect myself. Her sweet hazel eyes dim at my harsh tone, so I turn in the other direction to avoid her piercing gaze. Perhaps if I act angry enough, she will get the hint... but her determination, it seems, will not allow that.

"You should use a clean rag to stop the bleeding... it could get infected if you continue using that dirty one." Her voice wraps around me like a warm blanket after trudging through snow-covered mountains. She has no idea what she does to me—my soul bond, the other half of my soul, is a Human. What was the goddess thinking?

I glance at the blood-soaked rag and wince. She's right; this definitely isn't good. I should probably find a healer. The screech of metal against metal from behind makes me whirl around. She's in the forge—it's dangerous in here, and my treacherous mind can't help but worry for her safety.

"What are you doing?" I growl out. She's found the stack of clean rags but clumsily bumps against a pile of old metal trying to reach them. Even in her elegant purple gown, she somehow fits in my space—my dirty, ugly space. Without thought I reach to steady her and instantly regret it. The warmth of her skin courses through me, quieting the tension that builds when I try to avoid her. She looks at me with those beautiful hazel eyes and for a moment time stops. I drop her arm and take a step back, returning pressure to the wound on my hand. No, she needs to leave.

"I'm getting you a clean rag. You'll get an infection, like I said." Standing on her tiptoes, she grabs one of the few white cloths in the forge and dunks it in the clean water bucket I keep in the back. Her graceful movements mesmerize me, which is why I don't yell at her to leave right away. When she approaches, reaching for my hand, my entire being aches to stay this close to her forever. Her soft skin jolts me back to reality—I flinch away, snatching the clean rag from her hands and glowering at her attempt to help.

"I don't need your help." The annoyance in my voice is clear, though part of me fights fiercely to comfort her instead. Her face falls, sadness taking root inside her. I feel it too—the pain of pushing her away—but she's Human and shouldn't feel the bond. Though according to Emilia, even at the beginning she felt something for Timas, even if she didn't understand what it was. I can't bear the sadness on her face anymore, so I storm out of the forge to find a healer. The cut is deep and hasn't stopped bleeding; the new rag is already soaked.

Before I get too far, I look back over my shoulder. She's standing there, watching me leave, the hurt evident on her face. Guilt racks my body, just another reason I can't be with her, I am no good for her. Especially since she is a princess and I'm... well, I'm just a half breed. "Thank you," I manage to say. It's not her fault the goddess chose her, and hopefully this will be some minor inconvenience for her. My fate, a cruel and just end, is sealed.

One day she can find someone else, someone better. Even though every part of me rebels against the idea.

Stomping across the grounds, my next stop is a healer. I've been working with swords my entire life, can't believe I cut myself so badly.

***

The murky golden liquid in my mug calls to me, promising to drown my thoughts, but even ale can't quiet my mind tonight, can't quite remove the growing flame inside. The healer did too good a job—can barely tell I cut myself at all. This Fae magic confuses me. As an Orc, we wear our scars like badges of honour, proof that we fought and lived to tell the tale. Yet here I am, relieved to have this particular wound erased completely.

"To be injured by a sword I forged myself—embarrassing," I mumble aloud.

"There you are, you brooding green giant! You're scaring the kitchen staff again–those angry grunts of yours have sent more than one young Fae running to change their pants." Milori's voice shatters what little peace I'd found in this quiet corner of the kitchen. I should have gone to the lower city instead.

"I see your services as court jester were not needed. I am in no mood for you today, Milori." Wrapping my hand around the mug I down more than half the contents in one gulp. The bitterness distracts me for a moment before Milori sits across from me, smirk on his stupid face and his stupid messy hair. "You know there are these things called combs, you should try one out sometime. Might make you look less ugly."

Milori begins to act insulted but I know he doesn't need me to stroke his ego. "I'm hurt. I thought we agreed I am by far the better looking one of the two of us. Besides, the ladies don't complain about my looks." I stare down the man across the table, him and I both aware how much he hates the attention he gets from the women in this place.

"What do you want Milori? Don't you have some noble's ego to attend to? I know the kitchen staff didn't bug you because I'm sitting here *peacefully* having a drink." At the mention of said beverage I take the mug and down the rest of its contents, the buzz of the liquid barely touching the incessant pull of the bond. This stuff isn't nearly as good as it is back home. Tastes too good. Should taste more like dirt and burn on the way down. That is a good Orc ale.

"Well, as a matter of fact, I was told of your spectacular fail with your soul bond and your sulking behaviour here in the kitchen. Some occupants of this kitchen are afraid you are going to explode in anger and destroy the place." He mock whispers as he looks around at the empty space. Only a few people on the other side of the kitchen are quietly preparing the evening meal. I grunt in response, staring at the now empty mug which aggravates me. He's not wrong to question me, the longer I avoid Alette, the more I have found myself battling the darkness growing inside.

"I am very capable of controlling my anger unless an annoying little pretty boy shows up requiring a beating." Glaring at said pretty boy, he merely takes that as a compliment. Banging his hands on the table he jumps to his feet, grin on his face ready to say something stupid no doubt.

"A sparring match! Is that what you need to come to your senses about Alette? You're being ridiculous, passing up a chance at true happiness. I expected better judgment from you, my friend." His words start playful but turn serious, his eyes filled with disappointment. "I've watched you turn away from what could complete you. I can't understand it." He shakes his head, and I see the longing in his eyes—he who has waited so long to find his own bond, who understands the rarity and beauty of such a bond.

"You don't understand." I growl out, flopping back against the chair I'm sitting in. The squeak in the wood making a concerning noise when my bulk and weight already test its limits. Another reason I should have gone to the tavern—they have chairs made for Orcs.

Milori places his hands on the table, leaning in with a subtle fire in his eyes. I wonder if all noble Fae can show their powers within their eyes? I know Timas does, scary if you look at it too long.

"I understand enough, you thick-headed oaf. Your mom really screwed you up." Milori's stare challenges my own, asking me to say he's wrong but he's not. I clench my fists to relieve the frustration and anger that has lived permanently inside me since as long as I can remember. He's not wrong but there is no way I am talking about this... to him... in this cursed kitchen.

"Fine, let's spar. It'll make me feel better to punch that primping prince's face of yours." Milori catches the shift in my tone; he is always perceptive of the changes in others. Maybe he does it so he can protect himself, but it has made him a good captain. His eyes soften and then a glint of mischief surfaces.

"Alright, you grumpy Orc, time for you to see why the Fae race is superior." He pushes off the table, dusting his hands of some unknown debris and placing them on his hips.

"If I recall correctly, it was you rushing off to the healer the last time we sparred, had Timas yelling at me about 'breaking' his precious captain." I smirk at him and stand, the chair beneath likely very pleased I decided to move on.

"Hey! You ended up at the healers too—that broken arm was just as bad. Emilia yelled at me about breaking her precious little Orc brother." I come around and punch him in the shoulder. The smack sound echoes in the kitchen. Milori laughs as he heads out the back door while I try to get my mind straight. Maybe sparring will help me ignore Alette and the darkness even for just a moment.

Following him out into the practice yard, I watch him grab two wooden practice swords from the rack. The familiar weight settles in my hand as he tosses one to me. The late afternoon sun casts long shadows across the packed dirt, and a cool breeze carries the scent of approaching rain. Perfect sparring weather.

"Ready to eat dirt, pretty boy?" I twirl the practice sword, letting muscle memory take over. The familiar movements help quiet the chaos in my head.

"In your dreams, you overgrown troll." Milori drops into a fighting stance, that insufferable grin still plastered on his face. "First one to yield buys drinks at the tavern tonight," he says, and I grin at his arrogance.

Chapter 2

Alette

There is something otherworldly about waking up in Sonas. The birds sing with a joyful lilt, so different from the somber melodies at Gardenia Manor where I spent most of my life. Even the sky seems brighter here, as if happiness is woven into the very fabric of this place. Yet despite all this light, I feel hollow inside; a persistent sense that I don't belong.

A rap on the door pulls me from my thoughts, and just as I'm rising to answer it, one of the ladies' maids comes rushing out from my room's service area.

"I'll get it, Princess." Nilia, the Fae woman with kind light-purple eyes, hurries over to the large, imposing wooden doors.

I've asked her many times to call me Alette, but her 'station' according to her–doesn't allow such familiarity with nobility. Nobility... I can't help but scoff at the idea. Nobility implies importance; someone to take notice of, someone worth your time. As my father says, I am merely an instrument for the crown to use in furthering its power and reach. He likes to speak of it as some sort of privilege, but I know what I am and I know my worth. My value can be measured in acres of land, trade agreements, and political alliances. Each smile, each graceful curtsy, each demure laugh; all crafted since childhood to increase my price at market. A hundred thousand gold pieces in dowry, they whisper. The crown princess of the entire Human kingdom, they marvel. But strip away the silk dresses and jeweled crowns, and what remains is simpler: I am a signature on a treaty waiting to happen, a marriage contract with a pulse. Though I may seem valuable in terms of negotiating with the many dukes of the realm, I am nothing but a bargaining chip, carefully polished and displayed until the right offer comes along.

The sound of the doors closing echoes softly through the room. Nilia enters, carrying a tray laden with a teapot, cookies, and a small stack of letters.

"Princess, your tea," she says, her voice a warm and soothing melody. "It's a special blend from your homeland, along with a few letters addressed to you."

Nilia exudes a kindness that's become as familiar as the soft hum of this castle. Her blonde hair is streaked with silver, though her glowing skin and youthful energy make her age impossible to guess. I nearly fell over when she casually mentioned she was two hundred and seventy-five.

"Thank you, Nilia," I say.

She offers me a warm smile in return while setting the tray on the table beside my chair. I had positioned it by this window the day I arrived. The view outside captivated me from the start, and since then, it's become my favorite spot to sit and sip my morning tea.

The smell carries the scent of highland frost berries mixed with night-blooming jasmine, a unique and delightful fragrance distinct to Gardenia Manor's location in the kingdom—near the mountains, where the climate is cooler.

As beautiful as it is to look out onto the ocean, I much prefer the sight of the mountains in many ways. Emilia was kind enough to have a room prepared for me on the opposite side of the palace facing away from Windsmere, so I don't have to look at the place I've called 'home' for so many years.

Nilia pours a cup of tea and quietly returns to her duties, never one to stay and chat—though to be honest, I haven't desired to talk with many. Getting attached to anyone here will only lead to heartache, though I've found myself becoming very fond of Emilia.

Her friendship has brought more joy to my life than I've had in years. Timas has been nothing but kind, though he is still a terrifying and imposing figure. Milori has gone out of his way to ensure my comfort, and... and then there's Garrick.

I don't know what it is about that man that makes my heart flutter to life and brings an embarrassing amount of perspiration to my skin whenever he's around. Any glimpse of the hulking man with such olive green skin makes me swoon like some silly child. It's absolutely ridiculous that I'm smitten with him at all–and worse–he apparently hates me. He's been making that clear this past month, but something keeps pulling at me to go out of my way to see him, talk to him, or just be in his presence. But after yesterday, with that debacle in the forge, I'm not sure how much more embarrassment I can handle.

Picking up the cup of tea, I relish the sweetness of the highland frost berries and the warmth that it spreads through me. The envelopes draw my attention so I set my cup aside and pick them up. The top envelope is cream-colored with a red wax seal on the back. I know exactly who this is from... Placing the other envelope down, I focus on Father's letter.

I flip it over before pulling the wax seal off carefully, then allow the elegant red ribbon to fall aside. The letter is marked with the royal seal, and as expected, my father has had his words dictated... again.

> *Alette, it has been too long since you have returned home. I gave you time after that terrible situation to recover before travelling back home but it is time for you to return.*

Terrible situation? That's what he's calling me being kidnapped and dragged across the kingdom to blackmail him into fighting with the Southern Orcs?

> *It does not look well that the princess of Windsmere is staying in Sonas with the Fae. Although it was kind of King Timas to concern himself with your temporary discomfort, such intervention was*

hardly necessary. Your proper place is at home, not accepting foreign hospitality, however well-meaning it may be.

I write with joyous news—your betrothal has been finalized to Duke Roderick Blackthorn's son Bertram. This fruitful alliance with House Blackthorn will strengthen our family's power, particularly given the troubles we face on our borders as of late. This is not a request, Alette. You will return, and if I must send your brothers to retrieve you, I will—though that, as you know, would not be an enjoyable experience for anyone. But I am sure such measures will not be necessary. I will give you two weeks, Alette, and you will inform me promptly of your arranged plans to return.

Signed,

King Leofric

P.S. Your mother has fallen ill. The physicians speak of some mental affliction, or some such thing, but I thought you would want to know.

My hands tremble, making the paper shake slightly at the mention of mother. She may not have been entirely present for most of my life, but she wasn't evil like my brothers, or calculating like my father. She was not well before I was taken, and with her fragile mental state, I wonder if she has given up entirely since I've been gone. I imagine she's locked up in Gardenia Manor, hoping for my return.

Guilt begins to grip me. She has done nothing to protect me from my father or my brothers, but I always wanted to see her happy. I only have a couple of memories of her looking truly joyful, and most of those times it was just the two of us in the garden at Gardenia Manor where she found so much peace. Where I would often read to her and she could look at the new flowers the gardener planted. It was as if she was able to forget about the darkness and finally see light.

Those same birds chirp and sing, a cruel contrast to the fear that grips me. I fold the paper and set it on the tray, hastily wiping a tear from my cheek. I'm ashamed to say that I am more afraid of the betrothal than of the decline in Mother's health. Another reason to feel guilty. I knew it was a matter of time before he would arrange a match, but Bertram? Of all people... That man is renowned for his proclivity with women, and on many occasions, I have heard he does not care if the woman appreciates his advances or not—he will do what he wants.

I lean back in the chair and watch the sun rise in the sky, completely lost in my inevitable future. I don't have a choice; I must return. If he sends my brothers, I will not be able to say no either way, and although Emilia and King Timas have been kind to me, I do not wish to bring trouble into their home.

While lost in my thoughts, the second envelope catches my eye—sturdy brown parchment with a silver pin keeping it closed. My heart begins to pick up at the sight, and I immediately turn my melancholic mind to the letter in front of me.

It has been several days since I have received a letter from this person, and each time I receive one, I can't help but become excited.

Pulling gently on the pin, the paper falls open smoothly. The parchment itself should be rough by how it looks but it's not. It's soft to the touch and smells faintly of smoke and ash, a scent I have become intoxicated with since the first letter. A small pouch falls out from between the creases of the page, but I focus on the words I crave to hear instead.

My Little Ember,

You have plagued my mind again this evening. I saw you walking in the gardens and you looked miserable. If only I could have held you and pushed all the sorrow away, giving you the joy you deserve. Do not be sad, my little ember, it does not go well with your beautiful hazel eyes.

I was able to visit a village not far from Sonas. There I discovered a unique tea blend I thought you might like, made of Urdenia leaves, a lovely red flower, and rin nuts. The woman said it is especially sweet the longer you let it steep. I tried the tea and was not as excited about the taste, but I asked many others who enjoy tea to taste it and I am told it has a good mild flavour that settles the mind. Perhaps this will help bring the light back in your eyes.

Forgive me for not writing sooner. I'm afraid you puzzle me, and my deepest desire is to come to you and carry you off to a quiet place to simply be. But I know I cannot. Each time I see you, my resolve weakens, and I find myself searching for reasons to be near the palace gardens when you take your walks. My work has been left unattended as I write this. I will no doubt not hear the end of it but you call to me from the depths of my being.

I tell myself to stop writing these letters. That they only make things harder for me. Yet here I am again, ink-stained fingers betraying my heart's weakness.

Stay safe, Little Ember. And if sadness finds you again, remember there are those who would move mountains to see you smile.

Until next time,

The words touch a part of me I've never allowed anyone near. I should be afraid of such a letter. A lack of name attached to such words should frighten me but they don't, they make me feel connected to this person despite it all. Since the first letter—a simple note stating how I caught his attention—I have been enthralled by his words.

He always seems to know things about me, observing me with such thoughtfulness. The pouch of tea sits in my lap, and when I lift it to my nose, a sweet earthy aroma fills my senses. Maybe I'll bring this to the garden to share with Emilia later.

I hold the parchment close to my heart. How can words soothe such a sad, desperate part of me? And yet they do. Even if my future lies in Windsmere, at least I will have these beautiful words to find comfort in. They will remind me that, to someone out there, I meant something—even though to everyone else I am nothing but an instrument of the crown.

Chapter 3

Alette

"Who did you say gave this tea to you?" Emilia looks at me with a critical gaze, trying very hard to hide her smirk. It's been a lot of fun spending time with her, we've even been laughing and jesting with one another. I try to hide my smile behind my tea cup. I haven't exactly been telling her about the letters but I have been eager to tell someone about it. If I only have two weeks left to enjoy this life, I may as well take advantage of all of it.

"Well... um, I actually received it as a gift." Another sip of the earthy tea and I melt with how delicious it is. It nearly rivals my usual blend. Though, I am more partial to floral teas, but this one is special because he gave it to me.

"A gift? Really! From who?!" She has forgotten her tea entirely, leaning over and knocking her cup, spilling part of the contents in her excitement.

"Well..." The rush of finally telling someone feels amazing, to actually share this joy with another person, it couldn't feel better. "I have been receiving these letters over the past couple weeks and this came in the latest one."

"You're kidding!" She claps her hands together with excitement. "Okay, you have to tell me *everything*!"

Seeing her with such joy brings me to laughter. It is so freeing to see her happy, and the sparkle in her eye is encouragement enough to share more with her.

Before I can say anything, Milori approaches us, much to my disappointment. His smile is kind but that mischievous glint in his eye says he is looking for juicy gossip, "What are we so excited about, ladies?"

"Alette has been receiving letters for weeks! And... she just received the sweetest present!" Emilia practically bounces in her seat. A note of apprehension crosses Milori's face but there's no going back now. "Now shut your mouth, Milori. She was just about to tell me everything!"

I fiddle with the handle of my cup as I try to somehow hide in the large garden. Maybe if I don't say anything they will drop it... No, I will enjoy the last couple weeks of freedom I have.

"Well, a few days after arriving here I received a letter, hand delivered by one of the guards to my door." I cough, trying to clear the nerves from my throat, my eyes tracing the fermented swirls inside my teacup. "It was a sweet letter, about how he noticed me in the garden. It was beautiful, actually. It really made me feel seen." I can't help but warm at the memory of reading those words for the first time. "I've received several letters since then. Each one is beautifully written, but today he sent me something else. He noticed I enjoy tea and, while away from Sonas, found this blend... just for me." I can't help but get choked up by the kindness of it. I finally look up at Emilia and she is smiling, her face resting in her hands as she listens to my silly story.

"That's it really. I don't know who it is—he never signs his name." I rushed out that last bit because even though at first it annoyed me... I'm beginning to enjoy the secrecy of it. Besides, if I knew, it would be harder to leave and it was already going to be hard enough.

Emilia sighs wistfully while staring at me. "How romantic... A secret admirer here in the palace." A dreamy gaze covers her face and I can't help but also indulge in the intimateness of it. While I stare off into the garden, enjoying sharing something so personal with a friend, Emilia starts shouting, "Hey! Get your own cup!" She tries to smack Milori's hand but he is far too quick and swipes the cup from in front of her.

"Well now, I can't just let you ladies enjoy 'lover boy's' present without me!" He takes a dainty sip for all the energy he put into stealing her tea. She crosses her arms, playfully huffing in displeasure. "Mhmm, what a lovely and familiar taste."

His comment draws my attention and the apprehension is gone, replaced with a devilish look. "You've had this tea before?" For a moment I think maybe he knows who might be my secret admirer, a recognition in his eyes perhaps?

"I have, and recently. Actually must have been one of the blends I tried at the bakery in the lower city; she always has some of the most unique blends to offer with her baked goods." He says it hesitantly as if he is picking his words carefully.

"I guess I should visit her shop before I have to leave." The words float out of my mouth before I can stop them and Emilia whips her head around to look at me.

"When are you leaving?" She asks, concern written on her face.

I can't blame her, everything she knows of my home is not very pleasant. I slowly shrug in response. "Eventually. I can't stay here forever." It's something I've said many times before, hopefully she will let it go one more time.

"Nonsense. You know you can stay here forever. Timas has said as much, he knows I would have done something drastic to ensure that outcome." I chuckle because I have no doubt she would tell Timas exactly what to do. For such a small lady she has a great deal of power over the most powerful Fae in the realm.

She laughs, breaking the tension. Catching Milori's eyes, I can tell he doesn't entirely relax, even after Emilia has started into a story about one of the guards flirting with the kitchen lady who happens to be dating his brother. That would be awkward to find out. Milori's gaze is unwavering, assessing me. My only recourse is to drink my tea and pretend I am intently listening to Emilia.

***

The palace is all a buzz cleaning every inch as they prepare for the Night of the Golden Trail; hanging gold and silver decorations symbolizing the stars crossing the sky. I remember seeing this event happen once, it was beautiful. Apparently the Day Court celebrates this every two years. A special event where they dance and drink while wishing for a good future. If only it would work for me, but I'm afraid even flying stars can't stop what has been set in motion.

I weave through the many workers, glad most of them don't pay much attention to me. Here it's so much easier to blend into the background. I make my way through the busy gardens to this amazing section of the western part of the palace. A museum, I believe, with paintings, statues, and old weapons.

The further away from the commotion, the louder the clicking of my heels echoes off the walls. Massive, arched doorways sit at the end of this grand hall. The light pouring in from above changes colours as it reflects off the vibrantly stained glass. One door is slightly ajar, which is good for me because it looks heavy, and there is no one manning it to assist me if I needed the help. Not that I would want to inconvenience someone to do something as silly as opening a door.

Walking into the large gallery I stop in my tracks to take in the entire space. The walls are covered in images of noble or royal people all positioned to look regal and important. Statues dot the space with armours unlike anything the men at Windsmere wear. Weapon racks line the center, all showing the variety of Sonas blades. All elegant and delicate weapons that look beautiful but I know could kill in an instant.

I'm drawn to the right, looking at all the different paintings. I get to a section where there are several paintings of noble Fae women. It's odd, they all seem to be dressed with a matching pin to hold a sheer red fabric that flows elegantly from their shoulders. They don't look similar, so they must not be related. One of the women has black hair, while another has red, and another still has blonde. The blonde woman looks oddly familiar with sea green eyes and a smile that tugs at my memories.

"That's my mother." Completely startled, I shriek while turning around to see who has snuck up on me. Perhaps coming here alone was not a good idea. Milori stands a few feet away with a small smile on his face as he watches me settle.

"You scared me!" I place my hand on my chest willing my heart to slow down.

"I see that," he says before laughing. "What are you doing here?"

His question isn't entirely unwarranted but it takes me a moment to gather myself. I have become a little too comfortable with the group that lives here but I'm enjoying the freedom. "I was looking... obviously."

Milori comes up beside me to look up at the painting of the woman I had just been staring at.

I turn to gaze up at the image again, now seeing the subtle resemblance in Milori. "So, that's your mother?"

"Indeed. Beautiful woman, feisty too. Don't let that smile fool you. She was a tyrant when she wanted to be." His fresh laugh carries a stale hint of sadness.

"She's stunning." We stand there in silence for a moment before I ask, "Why do all of these women wear the same clothing, with the same pin?"

Milori takes a moment before he responds." In truth, I don't know. I have been here in Sonas–in the palace–for decades. I have tried to figure it out myself but the information has eluded me. All I have been able to gather is that these noble women were a part of something... Something very secret." His words are tinged with sadness and curiosity.

"Have you asked her about it?" Maybe I should just keep my mouth shut but apparently I am not doing that today.

He shakes his head slowly. "My mother always had secrets. She was also a woman who loved with great abundance. She is entitled to her own memories and secrets, even if it is killing me." I look over to see him smiling at me, the sadness gone for now. He waits for me to look at him fully before cautiously asking, "Now I wonder if I may ask you to help me."

"Absolutely! You have helped me many times... all of you have. It would bring me such joy to help anyway that I can."

"Marvelous," His usual rakish grin reappears as he clasps his hands behind him, "I need you to attend the Night of the Golden Trail with me."

My smile slowly fades as I remember I promised to go with someone else. "I'm sorry... I've agreed to accompany Lord Astralius to the event. He seemed rather... adamant I accompany him." If only I could have held my ground and refused.

"Ah yes, that pompous delinquent. Don't worry about him, I will encourage him to find someone else if you will accompany me. You see... I may have led a lady to believe I was interested in her. I was merely helping her find her way and she took that as an invitation to make me her knight in shining armour. If you accompany me she will be forced to stay away and... perhaps I can encourage Lord Artralius to occupy her time. It would benefit both of us." Milori almost sounds like he is begging me for this help, which is rather confusing. I have heard from the staff that Milori does not like the noble women's attention and avoids it if he can.

"Alright if you are sure it won't cause an issue. In truth, I am relieved to not go with him. He is very annoying when he talks about his cats." The memory of him describing in detail how he cuts up his cats' food won't be leaving my mind any time soon. This makes Milori double over and laugh.

"Oh how I wish I could have been there to hear that conversation. He is a rather fun man to antagonize. It's one of my favourite pastimes, in fact." We both laugh for a moment before all goes quiet again.

"Would you like to continue to look around? I can tell you what I know of the pieces. I am happy to be your guide today, if you wish that is." The tension that lives permanently in my shoulders loosens at the idea of learning and listening to all the stories. Excitement of hearing about the Fae culture makes the offer enticing.

"I would love that." With a smile on my face, Milori motions for me to continue into the gallery. He tells me all about the numerous nobles who line the walls before bringing me to the many weapons on display. He explains how each could injure a man, in far more detail than I probably needed, crafting a truly enjoyable afternoon.

Chapter 4

Garrick

These preparations only add to my agitation. Every mention of the Night of the Golden Trail sends a jolt of darkness through my blood—knowing Alette will be there with Lord Astralius makes my hands shake with barely controlled rage. The bond pulses angrily, a constant reminder of what I'm fighting.

"Ten minutes to board!" The sea captain's call offers blessed relief. Four days away should help clear my head, perhaps quiet the voice inside that's growing darker each day I resist.

"And where do you think you're going?"

I drop my head forward, rubbing my temples. Of course she'd find me. "What are you doing here, Em?" Turning, I find my sister—the Queen of the Day Court—standing on the crowded dock with a single guard. "Where are your guards? Just because the Night Court's beaten doesn't mean you're safe."

She crosses her arms, staring me down like she did when we were eight and thought she could wrestle me. The memory almost makes me smile. Almost.

"You're delusional if you think only one guard is with me. Timas has been particularly protective lately." She rolls her eyes just as Timas emerges from behind some crates. I should have noticed him—the bond's making me sloppy, stealing my focus.

Timas slides in behind Emilia wrapping his arms around her and kissing the top of her head. If I wasn't so absorbed in Alette I would make some comment about his public display but my skin itches to return to the palace while simultaneously desires to run away.

"What brings the king and queen to the shipping docks on this lovely day?" The sarcasm doesn't quite mask the strain in my voice.

"Garrick, you're being ridiculous. Why are you running away?" Emilia steps closer, her crown barely reaching my chest. I pat her head like I've done since she was small, grasping at some semblance of normalcy.

"Stop that." She swats my hand away, but her blue eyes—the ones we share from our mother—pierce right through me. "Now explain."

The guilt hits harder than any weapon could. "I just can't stay here. I need a bit of time. There is an order I need to pick up of white ash iron from the mainland. The king has commissioned specialty swords, don't wanna disappoint him." I glance at Timas with a smirk and he raises an eyebrow at me. "It'll only take a few days before I'm back. Five days, at most." I spit out, hoping the explanation of the timeline will appease Emilia.

She lets out a heavy sigh as she stares at me. For a long moment, she just shakes her head. "The day after the Night of the Golden Trail..."

Her expression hardens into a scowl. "I understand you're terrified. Everyone would be. But running from Alette isn't going to solve anything." She pauses, her anger giving way to something worse. "And the soul bond? Were you ever planning to tell me about that?"

The disappointment in her gaze cuts deeper than her anger ever could. I want to explain, to defend myself, but the words stick in my throat. How can I tell her what I can barely admit to myself? Speaking about the bond would make it real, and I'm not ready for that reality.

"You've been avoiding me too," she continues softly. "I know things are different now that I'm with Timas, but... Honestly, I've been afraid that's why you're pulling away from everyone, that it's not just about refusing the bond."

The vulnerability in her voice breaks something in my chest. We only had each other after our mother left—twice. What we forged through, that shared pain, should be stronger than this. Guilt claws at my throat, not just for Emilia but for Alette too. I'm becoming exactly what I fear.

"I'm sorry, Em. I'm not trying to run from you." I pull her in for a hug, something my Orc blood struggles against. "It's complicated. I'm not sure I can pursue the bond."

"She won't be like mother was to father," she whispers.

I tip my head back, fighting the surge of fear that has become a constant companion. "You don't know that. I'm not even a proper Orc, Em. Humans don't stay with half-breeds."

"I get it. You need time." She steps back, sadness etched in her features. "But if you wait too long, she won't be around and you'll lose her."

The thought sends a wave of anger and fear through me so potent I have to clench my fists to quell the rising emotion. The horn sounds off—blessed timing.

"It's unnatural to ignore the bond," Timas warns. "It could become painful."

I nod, already intimately familiar with the pain. What he doesn't say is what we all know—Orcs who reject their soul bonds eventually lose themselves to madness. The darkness growing inside me whispers that maybe I'm already halfway there.

Maybe I am running. But, I don't know if I'm strong enough to trust her—or myself.

"Thank you," I manage, though the words feel inadequate. As the guards permit entry, the docks are filling with people again, and our private moment is gone.

The gangplank creaks under my weight as I board, finding a spot along the rail to watch our departure. A Human boy races past, nimble fingers making quick work of the mooring lines. Just as the ship starts drifting, he leaps across the widening gap between the dock and deck, landing with a practiced grace.

Pride lights his face as he dusts off his hands, beaming up at the sea captain's approving pat.

The scene catches in my throat—memories of father's quiet pride when I first shaped metal into something useful, his weathered hand warm on my shoulder. Simple moments, before I understood how complicated life could be.

From the ship's rail, I watch Emilia wave goodbye with her characteristic enthusiasm. The mainland beckons, promising escape. As the distance grows between me and Alette, the bond's angry pulse reminds me that some things you can't outrun forever.

I focus my attention on the horizon and the distant shore. Maybe I am running away, the thought runs through my mind again and again.

Chapter 5

Alette

"I think this one would look beautiful with your hair." Nilia pulls out a plush pink gown that looks absolutely breathtaking, its silk fabric draping off the shoulders. While most people would be thrilled to wear such exquisite clothing, it reminds me too much of what I'm forced to wear in Windsmere. Always light and inviting colours to entice the eye, Father says. *Perfect for displaying his prized bargaining piece.* The thought makes my skin crawl, knowing that tomorrow I'll be back in those pastel cages, paraded before whatever noble father deems worthy this time.

Emilia spared no expense bringing dress after dress for me to try on. Maybe I should just pick this one. Nilia said it goes with my hair... though being dark blonde, almost everything does.

Walking over to the rack that was brought in, I start sifting through dress after dress, hoping to find something appealing, or at least something I can feel comfortable in. There are blues, purples, reds, and even yellows to choose from. All of the silks, velvets, lace-covered ones–they're all beautiful but just not quite right.

"So not the pink one," Nilia mutters as she returns the dress to the rack.

I don't mean to be difficult—I'm feeling uneasy about the evening and worried about returning to Windsmere tomorrow. Father may have said he would give me two weeks, but his latest letter 'corrected' my travel arrangements. I haven't even told Emilia yet.

Moving another beautiful gown aside, I gasp at one hidden behind a vibrant red dress. I pull it out from the mounds of fabric. While holding it up for the late sunlight to cascade along the length, I pause to take it all in.

"It's beautiful," I whisper. Dark green with accents of silver twisting down the gown, with small delicate stars dotting the sheer fabric overlay, adding to its depth. The bodice plunges lower than what I'm used to, but the sleeves fall elegantly off the shoulder, creating magic within the fabric—if that's even possible. The fabric is smooth to the touch, unlike anything I've felt before, and shimmers in the light.

"Moonsilk," Nilia says, and I turn to look at her, holding the gown in my hand.

"Pardon?" I ask, confused.

"It's called moonsilk, the fabric. Only found on a few Fae islands and only harvested twice a year. It can be coloured however the designer desires—in this case green. It's a beautiful colour, would go nicely with your hazel eyes." Nilia smiles sweetly at me as I look back at the dress.

"I'd like to try this one, please." Nilia wastes no time and helps me into the gown. The fabric lays beautifully on me—it feels nothing like the gowns of Windsmere which usually are stiff and agitating. No, this gown is beyond comfortable. The colour is what I like the most, though I'm embarrassed to even think of the reason why I have a new favourite colour, so I won't. I'll just enjoy it for what it is.

Nilia pulls half of my hair to the back and pins it with a large ornate silver star that matches the dress beautifully. She places a long delicate silver necklace with a similar star pendant around my neck, the piece complementing the entire outfit perfectly.

"Oh, Nilia, it's beautiful," I say, emotion clogging my throat.

"You are beautiful, Princess." She has always been so kind and generous with her compliments.

"For the first time, I feel like one." The words slip out before I can stop them and I slap my hands over my mouth, mortified I've allowed my inside thoughts out. I turn to look at Nilia, about to explain the slip, but she isn't judging me—she looks at me with kindness which only adds to the building emotion.

"Princess, may I say something?" Relieved she wants to speak, and I don't have to babble out an excuse, I nod my head.

"You are nothing like what I've heard of the Human royalty. You are considerate and kind. I could tell the moment I met you that you were already hurt, far more than what those dreadful Orcs did to you. I know I'm merely a servant, but from where I stand, I think you are someone amazing and should be valued as such. I want you to know that I'm very grateful to have been able to serve you these past couple weeks." Her words make my chest ache. Knowing that these precious weeks of being seen as a person rather than a possession are coming to a close; I can feel the tears track down my face. No one has ever said such wonderful things to me. It's as if she could see the parts of me that have been neglected for so many years.

Without thinking I throw my arms around her, pulling her into a hug. I try not to cry more but I'm unsuccessful. When I finally pull away, Nilia pats my cheek lightly while smiling.

"Now, let's get your makeup fixed before that captain of the guard shows up and thinks I made you cry! Everyone thinks he is so nice and funny but there is something terrifying inside him I'm sure of it."

I laugh at her comment for many reasons, but the idea that Milori is terrifying does seem laughable. It doesn't take her long to fix what my tears messed up and soon I'm pacing the floor in front of the window, waiting for Milori to arrive. While I try to push away thoughts of tomorrow's journey, of returning to Windsmere's suffocating walls—it's unsuccessful. Tonight, at least, I can pretend I belong here... even if one person in particular seems determined to prove otherwise. My eyes drift to the window, wondering if Garrick will even attend the celebration. Part of me hopes he won't—it would be easier than watching him deliberately avoid my gaze again. The other part... the other part wishes things were different, though I can't explain why my chest tightens every time I catch a glimpse of him in the distance.

Milori arrives once the sun has finally set and is ushered in by Nilia.

"Ah you look beautiful, Alette," Milori says with a bow. He is wearing a silk cream top with matching gold overcoat and pants. He looks very dashing, I can see why so many vie for his attention.

"And you look rather handsome." His green eyes brighten at the compliment. He turns and offers his arm with a graceful gesture. I slip my hand into the crook of his elbow, my pulse quickening with anticipation for the evening ahead.

Music drifts through the wide-open windows, mingling with the sound of laughter and conversation from the party's guests. The closer we get to the gardens, the louder it becomes.

My steps slow as we approach. In the few weeks I've been here in Sonas, I've found more freedom than in all my years at Windsmere. Here, I'm not just an ornament to be displayed or a pawn in my father's political games. The thought of returning tomorrow makes my chest tighten. I haven't even had the chance to say proper goodbyes.

I scan the crowd through the windows, searching for a particular tall figure. Despite everything in me saying I shouldn't care whether Garrick is here or not, I do. The way he's been avoiding me since that day in the training grounds stings more than it should. I've seen the way his jaw clenches when our paths cross; how he turns away as if the sight of me burns. Part of me wants to corner him, demand why he looks at me with such contempt. Is it just because I'm Human? The thought makes my stomach twist—I'm so tired of being judged for what I am rather than who I am.

Milori slows to a stop just outside the large doors that lead into the gardens. His brow furrows as he studies my face.

"Is something the matter, Alette?" There's genuine concern in his voice, so different from the calculated interest I'm used to from the nobles at home. For a moment, I'm tempted to tell him everything; about tomorrow's departure, about the weight pressing down on my chest, about how I'm dreading returning to being nothing more than my father's bargaining chip. But... I can't bring myself to spoil the evening with my troubles.

"Just nervous. I've never been to a celebration like this." My hope is that I am convincing enough he won't say anything but his eyes are too keen, too observant. After a moment's pause, he nods his head and continues to lead us into the gardens. I'm not sure what he saw but I am grateful he is not pushing the issue.

Everyone is smiling and laughing as beautiful flutes filled with an amber liquid are being passed out from gold platters to partygoers. The large trees have gorgeous gold and silver fabric hanging from their branches, and orbs of light float in the air, illuminating the garden. It's beautiful and magical.

Milori weaves us through the crowd, occasionally waving or nodding to someone I don't know while I desperately try taking everything in.

It feels otherworldly, nothing like the stiff and uptight events in the Human kingdom. This is... magical.

"There you are!" I turn at the sound of Emilia's voice. She is stunning in a silver gown that shimmers in the night like moonlight on water. Timas stands beside her in a matching robe, the silvery fabric making his black hair appears even darker by contrast. Despite his kind smile, there's something inherently intimidating about him—a reminder that beneath his courtly manners lies the most powerful Fae in existence.

Emilia grabs my hands and bounces with excitement. The bubble of laughter that escapes me is so freeing.

"Oh, Emilia, you look beautiful!" I can't help but gush.

"Me?! Look at you! Oh, Alette, you look stunning!" I feel heat rise to my cheeks. Many people have complimented me before, but to hear it from a friend—a true friend—makes the words feel genuine rather than the hollow flattery I'm used to. "I am so excited you're here tonight! If only my stubborn brother wasn't determined to miss this." The mention of Garrick catches me off guard. I guess that answers the question of whether he's here this evening. I miraculously manage to not show any emotion because Emilia goes back to talking about the celebration.

"Okay, let's go dance!" Emilia grabs my hand and leads us further into the garden.

"What? Where are we dancing? Shouldn't we bring the men?" I look over my shoulder to see Milori and Timas standing together, talking and drinking that amber drink.

"This isn't the Human kingdom, Alette. Here the Fae dance together and with their significant others. So you and I are going to dance. Then we'll get lost in the music, the Fae wine,

and the delicious desserts. Bilna made some of my favorites!"
Determined to enjoy the evening, I try to loosen my shoulders
and allow Emilia to lead me into the crowd.

The following hours are consumed by dance, laughter, and
eating way too much.

"I haven't had this much fun in... well ever." I mention to no
one in particular as we rejoin the group. A perfect way to spend
my last night in Sonas.

"My flower, we need to go do the speech before the stars fly."
Timas nuzzles Emilia, and I can't resist the pang of jealousy. To
have someone who loves you so unconditionally for exactly who
you are is a sight to behold.

"Alright. I'll be back," Emilia says to me, but I politely wave
her on. I understand royal duty—there is no way to avoid it...
even if you desire to.

"Sickening, isn't it?" Milori says, coming up beside me and
handing me another glass. I take the offered Fae wine and smile.

"I'm glad they have found each other. At least some in this
world can find their perfect half," I say wistfully.

"Come, I want to show you something."

Milori holds out his arm for me again, and I gladly take it. He
leads us out and away from the crowd, the noise slowly fading
into the background. We end up outside the garden, darkness
engulfing us.

"And where exactly are we going?" I ask Milori, curious why
we are so far away from everyone else.

"Away from the noise," he says with exhaustion lacing his voice. "I also wanted you to be able to see the stars cross the sky better, and it's better out here away from the lights—especially since it's your last night." My body freezes at his words. How does he know that?

"I'm the captain of the guard, aware of everything that goes on in this palace. You really think I wouldn't know about your early morning escape plan? Even if your brother is meeting you on the mainland it's not safe."

I look up at Milori. In shock, I don't know what to say to that, but also not surprised he knows so much. "Uh–I–um..." .

"Wow, that was exemplary articulation you have there." He snorts and I can't help but knock my shoulder into him.

"I didn't want anyone to know. I didn't want it to ruin the evening," I finally say while clasping my hands together in front of me, squeezing them to relieve some of the anxiety building inside me.

"There is no need to hide this type of information, but you should know that you've signed my death sentence. Once Emilia finds out I knew, she will have me hung from the tallest tower for taking her best friend away from her." He sighs. The stars in the sky are so bright they illuminate us both, allowing the dark of night to cast outlines along his body.

"You didn't tell her?" .

He turns to look at me, and though I can't fully see his features, I can tell he has a kind smile to offer me.

"It seems to me not many people are on your side. I did not want to break your trust by doing that. Though I did break the queen's trust... but she'll forgive me, she always does. Timas on the other hand may toss me into the channel." I huff out a laugh—from what I can tell from Timas and Milori's relationship, they have a very antagonistic one where throwing each other around isn't actually that uncommon.

"Glad to see you laughing, and smiling," Milori says while knocking his shoulder into me.

"It's nice to laugh." The stars seem to grow ever brighter as quietness falls on us once again.

"So, are you going to explain why you're returning to that bland and pompous kingdom of your father's?"

I contemplate for a moment, trying to distract him, but if this is my last night of true freedom, maybe for once I can trust someone enough to explain... everything.

"Father sent me a letter a couple weeks ago telling me I must return. He has arranged a marriage for me, and he expects me in Windsmere to fulfill my duty as its princess. He said if I didn't return that he would send my brothers, and well, that would have been unpleasant for everyone to say the least. I do not desire to bring my problems to Timas and Emilia's doorstep. I have enjoyed my time here so much, and I will forever remember the joy and kindness I have felt here. It's just time I return." My words hang in the air as Milori pushes out a long breath.

"Well, it's official—I hate your father." The sudden declaration catches me so off guard that I snort-laugh.

"You think I'm joking? I've never met the man, but I can already tell we will not be sitting down to play a game of shuck-ral," he says with disgust. "And I can play that with pretty well anyone."

"What in the realm is shuckral?" He just clicks his tongue and waves me off.

"It's a game that even an Orc can play, and they are terrible at strategy games. Anyways, you know Timas would protect you. You do not need to return. There is a place for you here."

Now I'm the one laughing, but it's not of joy but resignation. "There is no place for me here. This city doesn't need a princess, and even if it did, I don't know how to do anything useful. Unfortunately, my *place* is back in Windsmere."

"The court may not need a princess, but the queen needs her best friend. She doesn't make friends easily—she's a bit odd, that one." We both laugh because we know that's not true. "Honestly, it would be the ideal job: show up, talk, eat, dance. They offered me the position months ago," he strikes a dramatic pose, "but I just don't think the queen can compete with my beauty, so obviously I politely declined."

Milori has such an easy way about him, making people feel comfortable and at ease, but the fact remains–I can't stay.

"I see your mind's made up."

I hum my agreement, not entirely sure what to say.

"Well then, I will escort you down to the docks and make sure you are not alone on this side." The sentiment instantly brings tears to my eyes. The kindness of the people here is nothing I have ever seen. I am truly going to miss it. "It's time to make a wish—the stars are about to cross the sky."

Milori and I look up at the sky. One large blazing light starts to cross above us, not so fast you can't see it, but gradually, as if it looks down upon us. Another smaller one begins to move, and then another. The sight is breathtaking.

Make a wish. What's the harm in that, I suppose. As delusional as it might be, I wish that by some miracle I will get my happy ending–but in case that doesn't happen–I wish this night would feel just a little bit longer.

Chapter 6

Garrick

The sea air does nothing to ease the burning in my blood. The Human princess I have no right to want. Four days away from Sonas—away from her—and my body feels like an over-forged blade, ready to shatter. The constant tremors in my hands have gotten worse. Running was a mistake. The soul bond pulls at me like a physical force, demanding I acknowledge what I've been fighting. I grip the ship's railing until my knuckles turn white. The shore of Sonas comes into view, and with it the crushing weight of what awaits.

Half-breeds don't get happy endings. I learned that lesson watching my Human mother walk away, twice. The first time, I was too young to understand. The second time, she left Emilia behind—discarding her children like trash.

As the boat finally docks, I feel grateful to be back on solid ground. Orcs weren't meant for sea travel, though it's still preferable to flying with Milori.

The sea captain approaches me as I exit the boat. "I have arranged to have the crates delivered to the palace forge as we discussed." I grunt and nod in response, happy I don't need to explain again what I paid him to do.

Though I could pay to take a carriage or a horse to the palace, I think a walk up the massive hill will help me clear my head. A little more time before inevitably crossing paths with Alette. She seems to haunt every corner of the palace these days. The bond trying very hard to pull us together.

The guards at the gate nod as I pass. They've grown used to the queen's Orc brother, though I hear the whispers. Too Human to fit in with the Orc clans but too Orc to fit in with the Fae nobles–hard to find a place when you don't belong to any of them.

Voices from the stables catch my attention, enough for me to alter my path.

"Yes, apparently she went back to get married!"

The words stop me cold. My blood turns to ice, then fire. I don't know who this could be but everything inside me says it's important and I need to pay attention.

"When?"

"Just this morning! The captain of the guard escorted the princess to the docks early..."

I'm moving before I realize it, looming over the stable boys. They shrink back in fear as I demand answers, the only princess I know in this palace is Alette and she wouldn't go back to the Human kingdom willingly. The rage building under my skin feels different than normal—darker, more primal. The soul bond screams in protest at the distance growing between us, a feeling I have been desperately trying to avoid.

"Who left this morning?" I growl out, not caring at all how I sound.

"Th-the p-princess. From the H-Human kingdom." The brown-haired one stammers an answer out first. I'm breathing heavily now, fully understanding what he is saying. Alette isn't here—she has returned to the Human kingdom. Why would she do that?

"What marriage?" I demand. The fact that this is even happening enrages me. The other one with blonde hair responds this time.

"The p-princess is arranged to be married." He at least sounds better than the other boy who looks like he might wet his pants. But at this point all logical thought is gone, and my fear and rage have intermingled to become a perfect storm.

"To who!" Both boys' hands fly up as if to protect themselves though I have not moved. The intensity in my voice, however, shakes the very ground we stand on.

"I-I don't know," the blonde boy says, shrinking further away from me. I have to find my sister, she must know more.

I drop my bag in the stables, it now becoming an unnecessary hindrance, as I am determined to get to my sister as fast as possible. The gilded halls fly by as I run through them. Staff hurry to either side while avoiding me. I'm sure a large green Orc running through the halls of the Day Court Palace is a sight but

I don't care if I scare the tiny little Fae, I'm determined to find out what happened to Alette.

By the time I reach Emilia's suite, I'm barely holding onto control. The guards eye me warily but let me pass. I burst in, fear and fury warring in my chest.

"You let her go?!" The words tear from my throat. Emilia sets her book aside, her measured calm only feeding the storm inside me.

"What was I supposed to do?" Her steady voice makes my skin crawl. The darkness clawing at my mind wants her to rage back, wants her to fight.

"Lock her in the palace! You're the queen—you have that power!" I pace like a caged animal, hands shaking so badly I have to clench them into fists.

"And make her a prisoner?" Emilia's voice could cut steel. "Take away what little choice she has left, just like her father?"

"Yes!" The word comes out more snarl than speech. "Better than letting her go back to that arranged marriage!"

Emilia's laugh is cold enough to freeze blood. "Now you care? I warned you this would happen. I told you if you kept running, you'd lose her."

Something snaps inside me. The roar that tears out of my chest isn't Human or Orc—it's pure primal rage. The furniture trembles, and for one terrifying moment, I'm not sure I can stop.

Guards burst in, weapons drawn. The look of fear on their faces brings me crashing to my knees and I bury my face in my hands. What am I becoming?

"We're fine," Emilia commands, every inch a queen. "Leave us. And not a word to the king." The guards eventually concede and file out even though I can tell by their footsteps they do not want to leave..

Once we're alone, she kneels beside me. When she pulls my hands from my face, I can barely meet her eyes. The darkness is receding, leaving only shame in its wake.

"I'm sorry," I manage, my voice raw. The bond pulses like an open wound.

"Oh, Garrick." Her anger has melted to concern. "I didn't know she was leaving until Milori told me. But this—what's happening to you—it's worse than you've admitted, isn't it?"

I can only nod, staring out the window. Every breath without Alette here feels like drowning, and I'm terrified of what I'll become if I can't find my way back to the surface.

The door to the suite opens again, but not like before when the guards came rushing in–it must be Timas coming to check on Emilia after my embarrassing outburst.

"Son." Father's deep voice carries the weight of decades of battle. Even now, his presence fills the room with quiet strength rather than the rage that once defined him.

I remain kneeling, the soul bond burning through my veins like molten metal.

Father moves to stand beside me, his scarred hands clasped behind his back as he looks out the window. Though he traded his axes for a hammer years ago, he still carries himself like a warrior.

"When I met your mother, I thought I'd found something worth laying down my weapons for." His voice is gruff but measured. "I was wrong about her, but not about what she gave me." He pauses. "You showed me there were battles worth fighting beyond those bloody fields."

"She left us." The bitterness I've carried for years threatens to choke me. "Just like she left Emilia. How can I trust..." I clench my fists. "I'm not even a proper Orc. Too Human for the clans, too Orc for the nobles. What could I possibly offer a princess?"

"You think I don't see how you've been running?" There's an edge to Father's voice now. "The soul bond isn't about what you are. It's about who you choose to be."

"And if she's like Mother? If she looks at me and sees something to discard?" The fear that's been eating me alive finally spills out. "I've already pushed her away. After everything..."

"Your mother's sins are her own." He turns to face me fully. "But this magic—it's killing you, son. I've watched you struggling against it. Keep fighting it and you'll become something far worse than any monster you fear being."

His words hit like a physical blow because I know they're true. I can feel the darkness growing, the rage building beneath my skin. If I don't act soon, there won't be enough of me left to fight for her.

"What if I'm too late?"

"Then you die as yourself, fighting for something that matters." He grips my shoulder, his strength anchoring me. "Better than letting your mother's ghost make the choice for you."

The truth of it settles in my bones. Standing slowly, I meet his eyes. "I'm going after her."

He nods once, approval clear in his face. "You're a warrior's son, no matter your blood. Time to prove it.

I straighten my shoulders, purpose replacing paralysis. I'll follow Alette to the Human kingdom and fight for her—or I'll lose myself trying.

***

The docks are quiet this late afternoon. I am certain there's a boat I can hire to take me across to the mainland. Normally the best way to travel across the sea is to board one of the merchant ships in the morning, as typically they prefer the day to make their travels.

A few people wander around, some loading merchandise onto ships for tomorrow's departure. At the far end, a smaller ship sits anchored with a young sea captain tidying up. Hopefully he feels like going for another trip across the channel.

"Hey, you willing to take a private hire?" The young man looks up from coiling rope, brown hair escaping his wide-brimmed cap.

"Might be willing. For the right price." Sharp kid.

"Double your normal rate if we leave now." The gleam in his eyes tells me I've got myself a ship. Perfect.

"Come aboard." He moves with practiced efficiency, preparing the small cargo vessel. She's weathered but solid enough.

As I find a spot to wait, something inside me settles for the first time in days. The constant war between soul and sense quiets, replaced by a different kind of tension. Maybe my instincts weren't entirely wrong about pursuing Alette. Though the thought still terrifies me.

"Alright, let's set off." The sea captain's enthusiasm for sailing is obvious. I move closer, curious about someone commanding their own vessel so young.

"What's your name?" I ask, curious about this young man.

"Danny. Yours?" He turns the wheel to steer us out of the harbour.

"Garrick. Been sailing long? Haven't seen you around before." His face lights up—clearly I've hit on a favorite topic.

"Been sailing since I could walk. Grew up on boats with my father. He passed away a few years back, but I knew I had to keep his ship going." Pride and grief mingle in his voice—a familiar combination.

"If this trip goes well, I might have more work for you. I'm the king's blacksmith, always needing ore from the mainland." His eyes light up at the prospect. Good, hunger makes for reliable workers.

"Heard the king's fair to work for." The enthusiasm tells me he knows Timas pays well—one of the better attributes he possesses.

"Pays well enough." I lean against the rail, watching the horizon. A shadow passes overhead, and Danny's face tightens with concern. I recognize that silhouette with irritating familiarity.

Grabbing an oar from the deck, I test its weight. "Don't worry. Just a pest." The wood whistles through the air as I launch it skyward.

"Ah!" The satisfying yelp echoes down as the shadow veers sharply. I knew I would miss but throwing stuff at him always makes me happy.

"What is that?" Danny's voice moves from concerned to alarmed.

"Like I said—a pest. I'll pay for the oar." The shadow grows larger as my unfortunate miss allows its owner to land.

"Are you *kidding me*? An *oar*? You brainless Orc, I was *flying*! Do you know how much concentration that takes? I could have died!" Milori's outrage just improves my mood.

"If the king's captain can't dodge one tiny piece of wood, you're not very good at your job."

"You know him?" Danny whispers, eyeing Milori's disheveled landing.

"Unfortunately." I watch Milori adjust his clothes with excessive drama. Just what I needed—a babysitter for my rescue mission.

"What are you doing here, Milori?" I grab his bag and toss it at him harder than necessary.

"Making sure you don't do anything stupid." He catches the bag with annoying grace, though I don't miss the slight stumble he tries to hide. "Though apparently I'm too late for that. Stealing away in the night? Not your finest moment."

My deadpan response comes swiftly, "It's barely late afternoon."

"Details." He waves his hand dismissively. "Point is, you're planning something rash and ill-advised."

"How do you know! I don't even know what I'm going to do. Besides I'm going after her, isn't that what everyone wanted me to do!" The words come out as more of a growl than intended.

"Yes, but preferably not in a way that starts a war with the Human kingdom and with your amazing diplomatic skills," he says sarcastically. "You need someone who actually knows how to talk to nobles. Your grunts aren't going to get you very far." I can't help but scowl at him.

Milori turns to Danny, who's watching our exchange with wide eyes. "Change of plans—we're headed to Port Westcliff."

"What! Absolutely not." My hands ball until the green turns grey. "This is my ship."

"Technically, it's his ship." Milori points to the sea captain before continuing dismissively, "And since I outrank you..."

"You don't outrank me. I don't work for you, twinkle toes." This disillusioned Fae is just asking to get punched.

"No, but I speak for the king. Who—might I remind you—would very much like to avoid diplomatic incidents with Windsmere at the moment as there are some... complicated issues at play." I glare at Milori, taking in the shift in his stance. I haven't heard about these complicated issues but I haven't exactly been keeping up to date either.

Something irrational takes over me. The idea that Milori is coming with me to find Alette sparks a sense of fury I am not sure I can control.

"She's mine!" The words fall out of my mouth before I can stop them, the anger rocks the small ship we stand on. My heart is pumping in my ears and I know what I am feeling is irrational, especially since Alette doesn't even know my interest in her, but it's so deep within me I can't seem to keep it in.

"Yes, she is." Milori's voice softens, that look of understanding he gives and the shift in his tone is enough for me to get my breathing under control. "Which is why we're going to do this right. With a plan that doesn't end with you in chains or dead. *Or else Emilia is going to kill me.*"

His voice fades to a mumble. The captain clears his throat, drawing our attention to him. He flinches slightly when he looks at me but manages to control himself. Impressive. "Um, where exactly am I taking you gentlemen?"

Milori and I lock eyes, neither willing to back down. He obviously knows something I don't and, although where we were originally going is closer to Windsmere Castle, the bond pulses in agreement with his words. Running in blind will only put Alette in more danger and if there is more going on then I'm aware of... it would be best to know what that is.

"Westcliff," I finally growl. "But I'm not happy about it."

"Noted." Milori's grin returns. "Now, want to hear how we're actually going to rescue your princess?" I try to shake out the tension in my shoulders. This is going to be a long trip.

Chapter 7

Alette

M ilori was kind enough to bring me down to the docks so early in the morning. He didn't make me feel guilty about leaving but I could tell he didn't agree with my choice. In truth I wish I had a different choice. My luggage was loaded up onto a Human vessel sent by my father because the very idea of me riding on a Fae vessel was so abhorrent to the man that he ensured I wouldn't have to face such 'embarrassment.' He needs the appearance that he cares about me, but it's just another way he manages my life.

Port Westcliff comes into view, the busy port already filled with the usual morning bustle. Merchants hawk their wares from crowded stalls while dock workers load and unload cargo from ships of various sizes. The salty air mingles with scents of fresh fish, spices, and the ever-present smell of unwashed bodies that seems to permeate any Human settlement. Ships from across the continent bob gently in their moorings, a show of how much the kingdom relies on trade with Sonas.

With the ship finally docked, the sea captain ensures I am the first to disembark.

"Right this way, princess." The old captain looks rather put together with an official looking uniform, likely given for him to wear while escorting me to the Human shores. I'm honestly shocked that this is the ship I was to come home on. The one I had secured was much nicer but then again, never good enough.

The gangplank is laid out, a rope railing attached to help with balance but I don't need it. Years of practice in these shoes and tight dresses means I can be stable on anything.

My choice in attire was specially made in Sonas to fit the Human style and meet Father's high standards. Despite the fact I lost so much weight while held captive, I have gained a good amount back by just eating properly in Sonas. I am far healthier now than I have ever been and he will not be pleased by how I look, the standard of beauty here is much different to that of Sonas. The corset that cinches my waist further pinches on the side and how I wish I could be wearing the beautiful gowns of the Fae. I brought several of them back with me though I am not sure I will ever get to wear them here.

"Princess." A gruff voice pulls my attention. Two well-armed guards stand waiting for me—so begins the life of being constantly watched again. The first guard who spoke bows and then turns toward the docks, while the second follows behind me.

The sounds of the water lapping can't quiet my thoughts. Last night was wonderful–a perfect evening in fact–but there's this small part of me that is desperate to see Garrick. It is absolutely insane. The man doesn't even like me. Besides, the very idea of being interested in him is crazy; if my father were to ever find out I have an infatuation with an Orc he may lock me away. I have incurred such punishment before but perhaps he would make it longer since it is an Orc.

Ugh what am I thinking? He has no interest in me, besides I need to forget about all of that—my future is going to be challenging enough. I think I'll miss the letters more; they made me feel special and seen and I know I'll never read a new one again. Thankfully, I have the old ones hidden in my trunk.

"Alette." The sound of my name carries above the noise of the crowd, the voice a familiar one. Through the crowd walks my younger brother, Cedric. His striking features perfectly resembles our mother.

I walk calmly to him, maintaining the facade of royalty while in the presence of the people. The guard in front moves to the side as he races up to me and wraps me in a hug. Completely taken off guard, I stand frozen on the dock unsure of what to do. Eventually I gently pat him on the back, encouraging him to let go. He hasn't shown me affection in years, since he was a young boy. To say I am surprised is an understatement.

Cedric pulls back, a film of tears covering his eyes. I don't know what is happening here, I feel as if I have stepped into a different world.

"I am so relieved you are well! I have been worried sick since those green beasts took you away."

"You have?".

"Of course! We have been worried to death over you, especially Mother. She's not been well since the kidnapping." I feel a pang of guilt at the mention of Mother, though I know I have no reason to feel that way. "Now come, I have a carriage all ready for us. I even have your favourite treats packed for the long trip to the castle." Completely and utterly stunned does not even begin to describe how I am feeling right now.

Cedric happily walks in front of me, guiding me to come along. He's not the worst of my brothers, my eldest brother Rowan is far worse. It hurt the most when Cedric started treating me with such disdain because I spent so much time with him when he was younger. In fact, I helped raise him when our mother was not capable. The moment he turned eight, father saw fit to take him to the castle to educate him in being a proper prince... no longer allowed to spend time with me or Mother.

Over the years he became more distant, the young, kind, and sweet boy gone. In his place was another tyrannical brother, using me to further his own purposes.

The carriage arranged for us is one of Father's best. The show of wealth and nobility is a stark contrast to the hustle of the everyday, working person in Westcliff. Cedric climbs in first while the footman offers his hand for me to get in and I gladly accept his help.

"It's a relief to see you safe," he whispers. I squeeze his hand in response, grateful for the kind words.

After sitting on the plush red cushion I adjust myself for the long journey. Several hours of travel await us and I get to enjoy it in this tight dress with my brother, apparently. I wish it would have just been me and a few guards but I suppose it makes sense

Father wanted to ensure my safe arrival... or maybe he wanted to make sure I showed up.

We begin to move and silence fills the carriage. I look out the window watching the hills roll by, the only way to occupy my time really. Cedric shifts uncomfortably in his seat, which draws my attention. When I look over at him, he seems to be over-adjusting his jacket, his eyes darting between me and the fields beyond.

"Is something the matter, Cedric?" I maintain a formal tone with him. We may be siblings but we're not close, and haven't been for years. He may be the kinder of my two brothers but I can't risk getting hurt by foolishly trusting too soon.

"I... I want to apologize." My mouth pops open slightly at his statement.

"I know that your life has not been easy, and am ashamed that I played a part in contributing to that unhappiness." Cedric leans forward, dropping his elbows on his knees, regret filling his features. In my twenty-six years, I have never seen him look so remorseful. Something unsettling takes root inside me. What has happened since I left Windsmere?

Cedric must see the confusion on my face because he runs his hands through his hair and squeezes it in frustration. "I don't know where to start, Lettie."

I suck in a quick breath, tears rushing to the surface. He hasn't called me that in years. Not since he was a young boy and still living at Gardenia Manor. I grip the fabric of my skirt, unsure what to make of all this. Something is very wrong.

"Cedric, you're starting to scare me." My voice doesn't wobble, though my emotions are all over the place. He finally looks up at me, and I see a haunted look.

"For the first time in years, Lettie, I finally see. I finally see what they have been doing to you and the lies they have spewed." I swallow the lump in my throat as he continues. "I am ashamed. I believed the lies, but I shouldn't have. You practically raised me, and the things they said about you have made me a fool." Cedric seems to be jumping large portions of what is going on because I'm confused.

"Cedric, I think I need you to start from the beginning. What is happening? I have never seen you so distraught." Whether I should or not, part of my protective wall is lowering to him; he is so concerned. That part of me, as his older sister, wants to help him.

"You sent me letters every week after they took me to the palace." He chokes on the words, and I am beyond shocked. When they came to retrieve Cedric, when he was eight, I wrote to him weekly for years. He never responded. I assumed he never received them, much of my mail was monitored even then when I was fourteen. There is only six years between us, but after mother had him she was not capable of taking care of him. We had a nanny but I spent a lot of time playing with him and taking care of him despite that. I taught him to read and write, hoping I could stay in contact when I knew he would inevitably be taken to the castle.

I scoot to the middle of my seat, pushing myself off the seat slightly to grab Cedric's hands.

"I told you I would," I say just above a whisper.

"I found them in Rowan's room. Hidden behind some old books. He doesn't know I found them, but I read every single one." My heart leaps at his words. "After you were taken, the castle was in a panic. Father was irate that they got to you and were using you against him. Rowan said some horrible things I don't want to repeat, but when I was in his room, he told me to collect a book from his shelf that explained the art of negotiation. It got out to the public that you had been taken, so Father had to make a public statement about it, which forced him to comply with the demands of the Northern Orc Tribes until he could bring you 'safely' home."

My heart beats hard in my chest. "Father wasn't going to try and rescue me at all, was he?" I should know the answer, and it shouldn't sting, but it does. Cedric shakes his head.

"I know I have said some cruel things to you over the years, Lettie, and I can't express to you enough how much I regret what I did. I always knew what they said was wrong. That you weren't a spoiled brat and a woman needing to be 'put in her place,' but I felt incredible pressure to follow them, especially Rowan. He would talk incessantly about it. But deep down, that wasn't the Lettie who taught me to read and write. I am ashamed I was not brave enough to stand up to them." Cedric falls on his knees in the small space in the carriage. He grips my hands tightly as tears trail down his face. "I know you couldn't possibly forgive me, Lettie, but I am so sorry."

Utter devastation fills his eyes. I understand what happened, I understand why he thought the way he did.

"Oh, Cedric. I know it mustn't have been easy for you either. I am hurt, but we are a product of our upbringing, and we've not been given the best of beginnings. I-I forgive you, Cedric, but please..." Fear begins to flood my body. "Please do not let this be some cruel joke. I-I don't think I could handle that." To be even slightly vulnerable scares me.

He leans up and wraps me up in a hug. A small part of my heart heals. Maybe things will be a bit better if he is not joining in on Rowan's cruel jokes and threats. We embrace for a long moment, a part of me hugging the little boy I feel like I lost all those years ago, but we are both older now and faced with the reality of our circumstances.

Cedric eventually pulls away and sits back on his seat. The tension eases, and for the first time I find myself really looking at my brother - not as the boy who turned against me, but as someone new. He reaches out to hold my hand, gripping it like I will run away. He was always an affectionate child, and it would seem he still enjoys it.

"I nearly had to beg for Rowan to stay and let me come to pick you up alone," he says quietly. "I needed to talk to you on my own. What we are returning to is not great, I have to admit. But Lettie, I will try to help you as much as I can." We both know his ability to help is limited, but it feels good to finally have a sibling with me at the castle.

"Thank you, Cedric. I appreciate it." With the emotional moment over, we settle in for a bit and just talk about silly, everyday things, but his comment about the state of the castle is concerning. My only hope is that, in some of this, I may be able to choose something. But perhaps that is wishful thinking.

Chapter 8

Garrick

It's dark now, the sun having set a couple hours ago, the sparsely positioned lanterns barely giving enough light to illuminate the area. I pass the pouch of money to Danny, his weathered hands trembling slightly as he receives it.

"You did well, I'll send a contract to you once I return to Sonas. Speak to the harbour master; he will have the information you will need." I shake his hand and he grips mine with both hands, his gratitude pouring through the connection, a far more pleasant feeling than the rage and unstable feeling I have been experiencing lately.

Danny's voice catches, raw with emotion. "Thank you! I appreciate this so much. I'll work hard for ya. I promise." His eyes shine with an intensity that speaks of the weight of his family's livelihood. A broad smile breaks across his young face.

"I know you will. Now take that home to your family. I added some extra for dealing with him." I point a thumb over my shoulder at Milori, who watches our interaction with a calculated gaze.

"Appreciate it." He beams, climbing back onto his ship with a renewed sense of purpose.

"Well, would you look at that, he does have a heart! Here I thought your delightful brand of grouchy Orc was all you could show emotionally." Milori's snide remark was intended to aggravate me but the interaction I had with Danny has apparently melted a portion of my dark heart, so I ignore his comment for now.

"Well, genius, what's your plan? You added several hours to our trip and now that it's dark it doesn't seem like a great idea to keep travelling." Grabbing my bag I heave it over my shoulder and head in the direction of the stables. "No matter what we do, we will need horses."

"My plan is to, again, prevent you from getting imprisoned or killed. But it would seem we need to find lodging for the night. There, we can make a plan for tomorrow." Milori falls into step with me as we navigate the nearly dead harbour, a handful of people mill about but most everyone is likely at home by now.

"Fine, but then you need to explain to me why we went so far out of the way and what kind of trouble the court is facing."

Milori hums his agreement as an older man steps out from the small alcove beside the stable. "Looking for a mount?" His coarse voice speaks of far too many pipes and hard liquor.

"Two," I answer gruffly.

"What my friend here is trying to say is if you have two we would greatly appreciate it." Milori flashes that insufferable charm of his, though I can't imagine why he bothers. The old man grunts and walks into the stable as no further conversation is needed. "It wouldn't hurt for you to be more personable."

I scowl at him unsure of his motives. "I am plenty personable," I can't help but say with deliberate purpose. "And people don't need your flowery, courtly, niceties to get information. This isn't the Day Court, Milori, this is the Human kingdom. It's entirely unnecessary and will likely put more distance between them and you."

"How am I supposed to know that! I know very little about the Humans, besides what I've learned from Emilia and the tactical information I need as the king's captain," he says exasperated. "Though, I have always wanted to learn more about their customs. OH!" The empty area echoes with his excitement. "Maybe we can do something the Humans do! You know, to see how they live!"

"There's no time for you to be playing around, learning Human customs. We need to get to Windsmere," I growl, frustration edging my voice.

"Okay, so we will discuss this later." His casual demeanor is sometimes so frustrating, though he generally has good intentions. The old man comes out leading two horses, each strapped with a simple saddle. Handing the leads to Milori, he eyes me for payment. Swiftly I drop coins in his old weathered hands.

"Where's your closest inn?" I ask.

"Just down the road, can't miss it." Without much preamble the old man thanks me before heading back to his alcove located by the stable.

"What odd behaviour. Do they really say so little in a transaction? Normally I would be spending an hour at least talking to them about their family, or the market prices," Milori rambles.

"This is why you aren't sent on any errands; you take too long. Most people don't want to talk, they just feel like they have to when the king's captain shows up." Something like hurt flashes through his eyes and I regret how harsh I was. Milori has always been judged by his job or who his mother was. Very few bother getting to know who he is. Many of the noble women want to marry him purely for his status, not because of his character. "Look, I didn't mean—" Milori covers his hurt, throwing up a hand to wave off my comment.

"I get it. *Much to learn*," he mutters. Now I feel guilty for my harsh tongue. "Time to go!" He climbs up onto his horse, his easy-going personality back in full force. Sighing, I climb up onto my own horse, my bulk failing to faze the steed in the slightest–must be bred by Orcs. Surprising they have such breeds here, though I suppose we're close to the southern border.

Our ride is quiet but I am unsettled by my harsh words. Milori, as per usual, looks as if nothing is bothering him but I know he is cataloguing everything around him.

"Milori," I call out to draw his attention from the scattering of wooden homes towards me. He raises his brow in question. "I wasn't thinking back there I—"

The man holds up his hand to stop me. "It's fine, Garrick, we are good. You have a lot going on. I was able to talk to Zornak before I left and he explained what's happening. A rotten hand if you ask me but you are also dealing with the consequences of that choice." I give a terse nod, happy to move on from this.

The inn is exactly where he said it would be, just down the road. Milori and I ride in relative silence; I think we both need it. I'm wound tight from fighting the bond for so long, and he's lost in his own curiosity.

The building emits a warm light, inviting any passing traveler to stop and rest. After hitching up our horses, we head for the entrance. An old sign sways slightly in the wind, showing its age. The door creaks as we step inside, drawing several pairs of eyes. Some are slightly wary, and others barely glance at us–as though we're just another oddity in this Human town. A large, green Orc and a tall, powerful Fae.

Milori grins, looking like he's about to greet the entire room, but I grab his shoulder and steer him toward a table in the back.

"Would you stop smiling like that?" I mutter as he waves at a few locals who narrow their eyes at us.

"I'm just trying to be polite," he mutters, grabbing one of the worn wooden chairs and sitting down on it.

"Look, I understand you don't get out much but Humans aren't friendly to the other species," I mumble. Milori watches me carefully select my words. "You're also with an Orc and we aren't exactly liked in this kingdom–hated is more accurate."

"So, there's more prejudice here than in Sonas?" His brow peaks. This question is part friend and part captain assessing the risk we are in right now.

"Significantly. It stems mostly from the fact we are bigger and stronger than they are but another part is the conflicts that have occurred on the borders for centuries. We aren't exactly known for our warm smiles." I force a smile for my tusks to protrude, showing how terrifying we look to the Humans.

Milori nods his head in understanding. Before he can say anything more, a serving lady comes to the table flushed from running around the inn. Her eyes widen slightly when spotting me, but recovers quickly.

"What can I get you?" Her accent is that of a rural Human. I've missed the feeling of just being with normal working people, no facade of superiority, just someone doing their job..

"Anything warm and an ale, best you got." I toss several coins onto the table. She'll bring the good stuff if I pay up front. After grabbing the coins, her small smile becomes a sharp nod at the amount given. "You don't have Orc ale, by chance?" I ask, hoping this close to the border they might stock it.

"Sure do. Just got some of the good stuff yesterday, you're in luck."

I grunt in acknowledgement, happy to be able to drink something of my tastes for a change. She turns and heads to grab our order.

"You don't even know what we're going to be eating," Milori grumbles.

"There aren't a lot of options in small inns or taverns. Usually, in-season vegetables and local meat get thrown into a pot and they call it dinner. Humans who live outside the cities or duchies don't have a lot of variety, not that the king would let them have much anyways with all the taxes he demands. A greedy and corrupt man, not exactly looking forward to meeting him shortly."

"What? Even on the islands far away from Sonas there are always a variety of tasty dishes. How can they survive on such bland food?"

I raise an eyebrow at him, shocked by how a man of his stature is so misinformed. "How do you not know more?" I ask, genuinely curious.

The server comes back hauling two large ales in one hand and two large, Orc-sized bowls sitting on a tray in the other. With practiced efficiency she puts them on the table before politely leaving to serve the other patrons. Grabbing my tankard, I down half the ale. That familiar burn is a welcome distraction.

"We've had no reason to interact with the Humans." Milori falls back into the conversation. He slowly shrugs while picking up his spoon to try the piping hot stew. "Up until Emilia came around, and the seer told Timas to invite them to Sonas, their kind were just a nuisance. Most Fae people believe themselves better than the Humans anyways. Most of them believe they're better than their own brother," he spits out. One dainty blow cools his small bite of stew and he hums with enjoyment before taking a bigger bite. "But since Emilia became queen, Timas believes it would be good to have a better understanding of their customs and how they function as a group. He does not want to be so segregated anymore which I think is a wise move though he's going to have to fight many noble houses on the idea."

"Timas is smart, and many of those Human customs Emilia doesn't know yet, seeing as she was raised by Orcs." I say around my own mouth full of stew.

Suddenly the door to the inn bursts open. "Fire! Fire at the Millers farm and they're being robbed!" The entire inn erupts in commotion as some people run outside. "It's probably those accursed Fae at it again, burning our farms and stealing our food," the old man a table over says, grabbing Milori's attention. The charming demeanour disappears and the face of a guard surfaces. His body goes tense, shifting from relaxed to battle ready.

"What Fae?" Milori demands, standing abruptly, his commanding tone leaving no room for argument. The old man assesses him for the first time, noticing that the man in front of him has pointed ears but to his credit, the old man doesn't back down.

"There have been attacks by the Fae all up and down the border. Burning our farms and stealing our resources. At this rate many of us are going to starve during the winter, and the king is doing nothing to stop it." The old man's friend tries to quiet him but Milori got what he needed. He looks at me and I know we are heading to find out what these Fae are up too. So I leave our half-eaten food and we head out of the inn racing over to our horses.

The orange glow against the night sky guides us as we race toward the Miller's farm, the reason for our detour to Westcliff becoming painfully clear. We urge our horses faster, passing a group of Humans heading for the farm with nothing but farming tools—not exactly equipped to face Fae warriors. A woman's scream echoes through the air and my blood begins to boil. Whoever these people are, they won't be living much longer once we get there.

The silo stands engulfed in flames, casting wild shadows across the farmyard where several dark figures move. Their movements are too fluid, too precise—distinctly Fae. We dismount quickly, and I catch Milori's transformation from courtier to warrior in the fire's light.

His hands begin to glow, flames erupting from his palms as his eyes lock onto a Fae man loading stolen goods into a cart. The fireball forms and launches in one flawless motion, drawing a scream of surprise and pain as his target crumples. Three more Fae remain, and Milori moves like the weapon he is—a soldier honed for exactly this purpose.

My attention fixates on one of the raiders holding a blade to a woman clutching her child. Rage floods through me at the sight. Only a coward threatens the defenseless. Drawing my sword, I charge forward, my weight and momentum carrying raw power. The Fae turns at my approach, bringing his weapon up to counter, but he staggers under the sheer force of my strike. His graceful movements mean nothing against my Orcish strength. While the raider is dazed, I manage to pull my weapon back and drive the blade into his side.

In a painful scream, he crumbles to the ground. I scan the area to find Milori is locked in a fight with the last two raiders, the men amazingly dodging his attacks. Pumping my legs, I go for the raider carrying double daggers. I yell, drawing his attention from Milori just as he tries to drive the dagger into his side. With quick reflexes, the raider dodges my attack but as he tries to come at my legs, my blade cuts down his shoulder.

Milori's power surges forward, blasting the man ahead of him. The raider crumples to the ground like a discarded doll. His attention turns to the struggling Fae beneath my boot, whose desperate attempts to break free are nothing against my strength. With predatory grace, Milori drops to one knee beside us, his hand still pulsing with that eerie glow of power I've come to know well.

"Where do you come from?" The words rumble from Milori's throat like distant thunder. The Fae man writhes under my foot, his face twisted with defiance. Whatever pain he should be feeling seems distant to him, buried under rage and whatever's pumping through his veins.

"Like I would tell a Day Court swine anything!" The man hawks and spits, but Milori weaves aside with practiced ease. In the next breath, Milori's fist connects with the raider's face, drawing out a satisfying cry. I lean more weight onto my foot, grinding his chest into the dirt.

"You think I care what you want?" Milori's voice drops to a dangerous whisper. "I'll give you two options: you can choose death by being burned alive, or I might let the Orc kill you quickly. Your choice." I've never heard such darkness in Milori's voice—it sends an uneasy chill down my spine. His eyes burn with inner power threatening to spill out.

The raider finally shows a hint of wisdom, taking a moment to think instead of fighting. Smart man. I won't lose any sleep ending his life if it means protecting others from whatever scheme he's part of.

"I stand with the true Night Court, not the pathetic one that bowed to the spineless Day Court." Milori's jaw clenches at the insult, but he holds himself in check. I can almost feel the restraint radiating off him.

"How many of you are there?" Milori demands, but the stubborn defiance blazing in the raider's eyes tells us everything. No answers coming from this one. Milori doesn't waste another second—his fist crashes down, and the raider goes limp. As Milori rises, I see the courtier from Sonas has vanished, replaced by something far more dangerous; a warrior out for blood.

"You're not gonna kill him?" I ask. Milori shakes his head with a grim expression.

"No. Let the Humans have their justice, they deserve it." A woman's scream pierces the air, followed by more voices raised in alarm. The silo fire still rages. Without hesitation, Milori breaks into a run toward the flames. I follow, curiosity warring with concern.

Villagers form a desperate chain, passing buckets of water that might as well be drops in an ocean. The Miller family huddles together, watching their livelihood burn while others scramble to drag carts away from the silo before the fire can spread to the barn. My breath catches as Milori strides far too close to the inferno. The heat must be unbearable.

"Milori! What are you doing?" I shout over the crackling flames. The crowd stops their futile efforts, all eyes drawn to him. True to form, the mad bastard looks back at me with a wink.

"Just being the knight in shining armour." His familiar cocky grin is back, though I catch the shadow of strain beneath it.

What happens next is pure magic. The fire—his birthright as a Fae noble—begins to move around his hands, its angry orange transforming into an otherworldly blue. His movements become fluid, and the flames respond to it, abandoning the wood of the silo and curling towards Milori. Each gesture pulls more fire away from the structure, as if Milori can command it, as though it was not some wild, untameable beast.

The very air seems to thin as the fire diminishes, until nothing remains but wisps of smoke curling from the blackened skeleton of the silo. Beyond that, not so much as a scorch mark mars the surrounding buildings. The crowd stands frozen, myself included, trying to process the impossibility we've just witnessed. I move to Milori's side, noting how his chest heaves with exertion. That display clearly took more out of him than he'd like to admit.

"You're full of all sorts of surprises, aren't you?" I say, watching the villagers cautiously approach their ruined silo.

"Oh, Orcy boy, you have no idea." I look at him out of the side of my eye, and we both break out in laughter. The little levity is a welcome relief.

"I don't know how to thank you," a middle-aged man says to us. The woman and child from before stand behind him, shaking while looking at us.

"No need. It was the right thing to do," I say to him.

He gives a weak smile, the bruise on his face telling me he tried to fight those men. "Wish more people thought that way. We don't have much; all we have is gratitude." Shame colours his words, but I'm shaking my head before he finishes.

"You don't owe us anything. Just take care of your family."

He tips his head in thanks, but then Milori speaks up, "There is one of them still alive, over there." He points behind us. "You can do whatever you want with him." Milori tucks his hands in his pockets as the man tells some of the other villagers and continues to assess the damage.

"I could use a drink," I say to Milori, walking in the direction of where we left the horses.

"Not that stuff you ordered before—what is that, anyway? I think it permanently burnt my throat." I laugh because that's the best part of Orc ale.

"Pansy. But I'm sure they have some sort of fruit juice for your delicate palate."

We laugh and head back to the inn. An ale and bed sound like a dream right now, though my skin itches to be with Alette. I need a level head, and that starts with some sleep.

Chapter 9

Alette

I stare at my reflection in the ornate vanity mirror, trying to recognize the woman looking back at me. The familiar trappings of my Windsmere bedchamber surround me–the intricately carved four-poster bed draped in heavy brocade, the towering armoire filled with gowns in my father's preferred pastels, the delicate writing desk where I once penned fanciful stories as a child. But now it all feels hollow, a gilded cage meant to confine and shape me.

The lace-trimmed silk dressing gown perfectly complements my carefully arranged hair to feel like a costume, a reminder that I'm back to playing a role in my father's never-ending chess match of power and politics. Every piece of furniture, every scrap of fabric, seems designed to mold me into the perfect princess, the prized pawn to be traded for alliance and influence.

"Would you like me to do a braid today, Princess?" Corrine asks gently, the usual playful spirit subdued as she senses my melancholy. Corrine has always been a wonderful confidant for anytime I was summoned to the castle. She is kind, and a bit

sassy at times, which on many occasions brightened my mood
when something in this awful place has gone wrong.

"No, I think a simple chignon will do. Father prefers when he
can see my face." The words taste bitter on my tongue. Hard to
believe that I was living a free life in Sonas not two days ago.
But it all feels worse when I think about it so I try to push it
out of my mind. Especially because every time I think of Sonas
I think of him. No, I can't.... Corrine's eyes meet mine in the
mirror, full of understanding. She has seen what I have had to
go through for years–but much like me she can do nothing to
change it.

"As you wish." Her deft fingers begin pinning and twisting
my hair into an elegant knot at the nape of my neck.

I focus on the familiar motions, letting them ground me.
Corrine has been my lady's maid since I was old enough to be
summoned to the castle to attend parties and gatherings. The
only gift my mother fought for was to ensure I had a trustworthy
ladies maid.

"I heard the Duke of Blackthorn arrived late last night," Corrine says delicately. "Along with his son, Lord Bertram." Her
words are carefully placed, and I note it in my mind as this is
one of the ways I get my information.

"Is it possible they will be at breakfast this morning?"

Her complacent shrug makes my stomach drop. I had hoped
I would be able to put off speaking with them for a little while,
just so I could get my feet back at court, but of course Father had

other ideas. Likely to ensure I am reminded of my place and to prove to Duke Blackthorn I am actually here.

"So the festivities begin," I mutter. Corrine's hands still for a moment, giving my shoulder a sympathetic squeeze.

"You have more strength than they know," she whispers fiercely. "Don't let them break you."

Tears prick my eyes but I blink them back. She's right—I survived abduction, survived this court for twenty-six years... I can survive breakfast with my father and future husband.

"Thank you, Corrine."

I stand, letting her help me into a morning dress of pale pink silk, another of Father's preferred colors for me. Delicate, feminine, everything I am to embody. Corrine finishes tying up my dress and adjusting one more pin in my hair. She turns me towards the mirror with a flourish.

"There, prettiest princess in all the land, as usual. Those poor nobles won't stand a chance."

I can't help but laugh at her playful tone. "I think you may be slightly biased."

"Never," she gasps in mock offense. "I am the very picture of objectivity."

Our laughter is interrupted by a sharp knock at the door. We both look at each other, unsure who it might be. Corrine walks towards the door opening it to reveal Cedric, looking stiff and formal in his crimson doublet.

"Good morning, Lettie, Corrine." He nods to each of us. "I was hoping I could escort you to breakfast." There's an undercurrent of nervousness in his voice.

I glance at Corrine, who gives me an encouraging nod. Having Cedric by my side facing Father and Bertram would be a welcome change.

"I'd like that, thank you." With one more adjustment to my dress I make my way to him. Taking his offered arm, I notice how he stands a bit taller at my acceptance.

"You look lovely," he says quietly as we make our way down the hall. He is deliberately walking slowly, which I appreciate. I'm in no rush to get to the dining hall. "Though I know that doesn't make any of this easier." His voice is laced with compassion.

"No, but having family with me helps." I squeeze his arm gently, appreciating his effort. After what he said yesterday I still wondered if it was all for show. But with him showing up this morning... I feel better knowing he is actually going to do what he promised; help me.

He covers my hand with his. "I meant what I said, Lettie. I'm going to do better, be better. You're not alone in this anymore." A warmth floods my body at his words, like a hug I've been desperate for.

Tears threaten again but I blink them back as we approach the dining room doors. I have no idea what awaits me on the other side, but for the first time in a long time I feel a flicker of hope that maybe, just maybe, I can face it standing tall.

Cedric and I enter the grand dining hall. I can't help tightening my grip on his arm as we draw everyone's attention. The room is warm and the smell of delicious food lingers in the air. The space itself is beautifully decorated to show the wealth of the kingdom. Large portraits of my father cover the wall, all in various poses and attire. Apparently having only one large painting wasn't enough.

Father sits at the head of the long ornate table, imposing in his deep purple robes. His auburn hair is perfectly shaped though the grey colouring the edge shows he is aging. Crown Prince Rowan eyes us suspiciously as we approach, his hair and sharp features a mirror of Father's younger self. His stare causes a chill to pass through me, he does not look at me with happiness after being gone for so long but rather contempt at my very existence.

Duke Blackthorn and Lord Bertram rise from the table as we enter. The duke is a broad, barrel-chested man with a graying beard. His look of disinterest is somewhat surprising. Bertram, on the other hand, is tall and lean with a hungry look that makes my skin crawl. From what little I have interacted with him, I know he is a disgusting man. I'm just hoping that he'll eventually ignore me once all of this is done.

As I move to take a seat on my fathers left side, Bertram steps forward eagerly with a clear intention of coming near me. "Princess Alette, it is nice to see you safe. Please allow me the honor of—"

Before he can finish his thought, Cedric straightens his back and speaks with an authority I didn't know he had. "It would be improper for my sister to sit beside anyone but family at this stage of the betrothal."

Anger and annoyance flare to life in Bertram's eyes but he controls them quickly. Cedric deftly guides me to my chair and takes the seat beside me for himself. Relief and gratitude fill me at Cedric keeping his word. Rowan's eyes narrow at Cedric's boldness. The duke looks to Father with a raised brow, but Father simply nods.

"You understand the importance of propriety, Alistair. Let the young ones be mindful of it." As if that was Father's intention all along, but I know otherwise.

The duke acquiesces, but tension crackles between my brothers. I squeeze Cedric's hand under the table in silent gratitude as servants begin bringing in our meal. At least I won't be fed to the wolves just yet. As we eat, Father addresses the duke. Their conversation is nothing more than glorified gossip masquerading as politics. Stabbing one of the potatoes on my plate, I stop nearly half way to my mouth as Father says something interesting.

"Alistair, your support in these trying times is most appreciated. The border tensions grow ever more concerning." Father takes a bite of his food casually as if their conversation is just addressing the weather change. Being mindful that my potato hangs in the air I place it in my mouth and chew slowly to hear what comes next.

The duke nods gravely. "Of course, Your Majesty. Black-thorn's men and resources are yours to command. The luxury of our families uniting." The mention of my betrothal sours the food in my mouth. "These Fae attacks grow bolder by the day. They must be dealt with swiftly if there is any hope to keep the Orcs at bay."

Father takes a sip of wine. "Indeed. Why, just yesterday I spoke with King Timas himself. I informed him that he needs to be looking into the incidents. It is not right that we deal with his miscreants when he is capable of dealing with them himself."

I try to hide my surprise. Father, talked to Timas? Highly unlikely, and even more so was Father demanding anything from him... If this is Father trying to show his supposed influence, I fear what Timas will do once he discovers it.

Briefly looking up from my plate I catch Bertram's eye, he looks at me with a barely veiled lust. His smirk stands as a promise of what will come and what he desires. My stomach twists with disgust. This person is nothing more than a depraved soul looking for his next selfish indulgence.

I refocus my attention on my plate, now with a fleeting appetite. Cedric notices Bertram's stare, and my unease, so he draws Bertram into a discussion on the current parties of the season and the ones he's looking forward to. I am most grateful for his stare to be somewhere other than on me.

"The engagement ball will take place tomorrow, Alette," Father mutters, his first acknowledgement of me since arriving home. If he was ever concerned about my well being he didn't show it when I arrived yesterday or even this morning at breakfast.

"Yes, Father." I say softly, acknowledging the party that will be the beginning of my new nightmare.

As the meal draws to a close, I set down my fork, eager to escape. "If you'll excuse me, I should begin preparations for the engagement ball. I'm sure it will be a grand affair."

Father nods. "Yes, indeed it will. No expense has been spared for this momentous occasion." He looks at me then making absolutely sure I understand this is important. "I expect you to be the picture of a blushing bride-to-be."

"Of course, Father." I start to rise, but Bertram speaks up, which halts my ascension.

"Perhaps the princess and I could have some time alone before the ball? To get better acquainted." His suggestive tone makes my skin crawl and it is not missed by anyone in the room. Rowan smirks at my discomfort and Father just looks annoyed by the change in subject. My heart begins to pump and fear takes hold of me. The idea of spending any time alone with this man seems unbearable even if it's an inevitable scenario.

"It would be highly improper for you to be alone with my sister before the formal engagement. Surely you understand the importance of reputation," Cedric intercedes, drawing a harsh look from both Bertram and Rowan.

"Cedric is right. I will need the entirety of today and tomorrow to ensure I am looking my best for you, my lord. I would hate to disappoint you." The pounding in my chest has made its way up to my ears. My hope is that this is reason enough to let me go on my way.

Bertram's eyes rake over me in a way that makes me feel exposed. "I'm certain that would be impossible, Princess." He licks his lips in a suggestive way but the arrogance of the man is enough for him to think about what I said. "I look forward to our time in the future." I don't miss the undertone in his voice but I force a smile anyway.

"You're too kind. If you'll excuse me." I dip into a quick curtsy and walk as quickly as is appropriate out of the great dining hall.

As soon as I'm out of sight, I practically run to my chambers. The guards watching me race the halls will without a doubt share this with my father but I need to put as much distance between him and I as quickly as possible. Once in my room I bolt the door and lean against it, letting out a shaky breath. My skin crawls with the memory of Bertram's gaze. Lifting my hands into the air they shake uncontrollably, I put them together in the hopes it will quell the shaking.

"Corrine!" I call and with quick speed she is in the room looking at me, concern etching her face.

She comes up to me, rubbing my arms to bring warmth back to it. "What happened?"

"I can't believe that is who my father arranged to marry me." I spit out. Understanding dawns on her face; Bertram is known across the kingdom for his inappropriate behaviour.

"Draw me a bath? Please?" The words sound weak to my own ears but in this small safe space I need to let go.

"Of course, Princess." Corrine rushes to get a hot bath ready for me. I move to the large window that overlooks the valley while I wait. My heart begins to slow and my breathing levels out.

The sun rises in the sky, shining its light on the many fields and towns from here to the sea. From this window you can just barely see the splashing waters, a sight I have always taken comfort in.

The blue eyes of a certain blacksmith race to my mind and for a moment I let myself relish the idea of him, even if it is completely made up in my mind. There were many nights I dreamed of what it would be like to be held by his strong arms, cradled in his protective embrace.

Though I'm certain he's not interested in me... my heart is convinced otherwise. A deep longing pulls at my chest, as if it is calling me to go and find him.

Ridiculous.

"It's ready, Princess." Corrine's kind voice breaks me from my thoughts.

"Thank you, Corrine." I try to put as much gratitude into my voice as possible. I can at least dream, even just for a while, but right now I want to burn the feeling of Bertram's eyes off me and then after that I need to write some letters.

If I am to survive this I'll need to reach out to what few allies I have here at the castle and in the kingdom.

Chapter 10

Garrick

The morning light filters through the grimy window of the inn, rousing me from a fitful sleep. Even in rest, my mind chases images of Alette–her smile, her laugh, the way her eyes sparkle in the sun. The bond pulses incessantly, demanding I close the distance between us. I was an idiot for fighting this.

"Rise and shine, you brooding green giant!" Milori's far too cheerful voice grates against my ears. Of course he's already dressed and armed, looking annoyingly put-together despite sleeping in this dump. "Though I suppose there wasn't much sleeping happening with all that thrashing about. Do Orcs normally wrestle invisible enemies in their sleep, or is that just your special talent?"

I grunt and force myself up, the flimsy blanket falling aside. "Some of us actually need rest, peacock. We can't all preen ourselves awake."

"Ah, but preening is an art form." He fastens his sword belt with practiced grace. "One you could benefit from learning, by the way. Your snoring nearly brought down the roof."

I make my way to the washbasin to splash cold water on my face. The bond's restless energy makes my skin crawl with the need to move, to act... To get to her.

"If you're done admiring yourself," I growl while drying my face with a rough towel, "we should get moving."

"Oh, someone's extra grumpy this morning." Milori leans against the wall, arms crossed. "Here I was trying to decide if I should be gentle with you, given your clearly disturbed rest. Tossing and turning like a love-sick teenager..."

The towel flies from my hand straight at his head. He dodges with that insufferable grin of his, but at least it shuts him up, for now.

Milori's laughter echoes down the hall as he exits, finally giving me a moment of peace. Looking down at my blood and dirt-covered shirt from yesterday's fight, I know it won't do. I grab another from my bag—just as worn, marked with burns and stains from countless hours at the forge. The familiar fabric settles over my shoulders like armor.

Catching my reflection in the grimy window, I study my green skin and the small tusks that mark me as neither fully Orc nor Human. A princess deserves better than a half-breed blacksmith. But the bond pulses through my blood like molten metal, demanding I face this. Even if she rejects me—and she should, after how I pushed her away—at least I'll die knowing I finally had the courage to tell her the truth. Whatever comes after, I'll accept it. I owe her that much.

Meeting Milori in the stables, I clench my fists against the bond's insistent pulse under my skin. He tosses me a bag without comment, though his knowing look says enough.

Inside is breakfast—bread and dried meat. Of course the pampered Fae thought ahead. "Figured you'd want to skip the inn's cooking and get moving," he says, adjusting his saddle straps.

I grunt my thanks and tear into the bread. By the time I finish, the horses are ready. "We'll reach Windsmere by nightfall," Milori says, swinging onto his mount. "The castle guards should welcome a Day Court emissary, even at that hour."

"And you're sure this plan of yours will actually work?" Playing diplomat sounds risky compared to my idea of working through the local forge, but it would save time.

"Already cleared it with Timas." He pulls out one of those mysterious Fae message orbs. "After last night's excitement, he's concerned about these rebels. Thinks the king knows more than he's sharing." Milori's face hardens. "He wants us to investigate while we ensure Alette arrived safely."

We urge our horses forward. Say what you will about Timas, but he looks after his people—and those who aren't. It's why I respect him.

"This mission just got more complicated," Milori adds, his military authority bleeding through his usual lightness. The rebels clearly trouble him more than he's letting on.

I nod grimly. Coming to the Human kingdom is turning out to be far from simple.

Time seems to pass slowly as we ride on. It's midday by the time we approach a small village.

"We should stop here," I grumble. Milori nods, but instead of taking the bypass road, he steers toward the main street.

We could have stopped at the stream that curves around the village, but that mischievous glint in Milori's eyes tells me we're about to do more than just rest for an hour.

"I hear music." His face lights up like an excited child's, making my eyes roll.

"No." I don't care what kind of plan he has, it's bad.

"But Garrick!" He brings his horse alongside mine, wearing the same pleading expression that makes the court ladies swoon. "When will I get another chance to see real Human culture? Look at all the people!" He gestures toward the stream of villagers heading to what appears to be a harvest festival.

"We don't have time for this." The bond pulsing uncomfortably, urging me onward. But Milori's enthusiasm is hard to resist, especially after how he helped at the farm last night and how I treated him earlier.

"One hour." He holds up a finger. "Just enough time to see what makes Humans celebrate. Besides, you look like you're about to break that poor horse's back with all that tension. When's the last time you actually enjoyed yourself?"

I grunt, but he's not entirely wrong. "Fine. One hour. But then we're riding straight through to Windsmere."

His face lights up. "Yes! I promise you won't regret this. Maybe we'll even find your sense of humour buried under all that brooding."

I swing halfheartedly at his head, but he ducks away laughing.

We find a stable near the entrance of the town and rest our horses there. Tossing the stableboy a few extra coins, he eagerly takes charge of the mounts. Milori practically vibrates with excitement as we follow the music and laughter to the centre of town. The festival is in full swing, with stalls selling everything from harvest ales to hand-crafted goods. Children run past with painted faces, and the air is thick with the smell of roasting meat and fresh bread.

"Look at all this!" Milori bounces on his feet, drawing curious stares from the villagers. His height and pointed ears mark him clearly as Fae, but his genuine excitement seems to put them at ease. "What's that they're throwing over there?"

I follow his gaze to where some village men are competing in an axe-throwing contest. A grin tugs at my lips despite myself. "Want to try your luck, pretty boy?"

His eyes narrow at the challenge. "Oh, you're on, moss brain."

A small crowd gathers as we approach the axe-throwing range. Three wooden targets stand about twenty paces away, rings carved into their weathered surfaces. The villagers part slightly, eyeing my green bulk with wariness that shifts to curiosity as Milori flashes his winning smile.

"Two throws each?" Milori suggests while testing the weight of one of the axes.

I grab my own, the familiar heft settling into my palm. "Ladies first."

His first throw splits the air with deadly accuracy, thudding into the inner ring. The crowd murmurs appreciatively. My throw follows, landing a hair's breadth from his. His second throw strikes dead center, drawing cheers from the onlookers.

"Beat that, you walking tree," he taunts.

My final throw feels off the moment it leaves my hand. It still hits the target, but not center like his.

"Pure luck," I grumble as the villagers congratulate him. "The sun was in my eyes." I half heartedly say knowing full well he did a better job.

"Of course it was." His grin widens impossibly far as he spots something else. "Look! They're using ropes and pulleys to lift people into the air!"

Sure enough, a contraption among wooden beams hoists laughing villagers skyward. I shake my head adamantly. "Absolutely not."

"Oh come on, it looks fun!" He stands tall, hands on his hips watching the contraption throw another stupid Human up into the air. I don't even try to keep the look of disbelief off my face when I look at Milori.

"You can literally fly. Why would you need that death trap?" I think my question is completely reasonable but sometimes I just don't understand him because even his answer shocks me.

"Because it's different!" He's already heading in the direction of the death trap as I shake my head in disbelief. "Your loss!" he hollers back as several villagers stare at the obviously insane Fae getting in line.

I walk closer but plant my feet firmly on solid ground as I watch him get strapped in. His delighted whoops quickly turn to panic as the contraption jerks him higher.

"Wait, wait! This isn't quite what I—AHHH!" Milori flails as the rope swings him sideways. "Garrick! This thing is possessed! Get me down!" his screams just add to the ridiculousness of this entire thing.

I double over laughing as the mighty captain of the guard dangles helplessly in the air by ropes and pulleys. "What's wrong, pretty boy? Not enjoying your cultural experience?" Should I poke fun, likely not but it's too good not to do.

"This is *not* funny!" His voice cracks as he spins in a circle. "By the sun, why do Humans do this for fun?!" His cries have gathered a crowd of people, their laughter only adding to the delight of this situation.

"You wanted authentic Human entertainment," I manage to say between fits of laughter. Tears stream down my face as he lets out another undignified yelp.

"I can fly! This is completely different! There's no *control*!" His legs kick wildly as the rope drops him a few feet. "When I get down from here—" His words trail off as the person in control of the system yanks him higher and with more enthusiasm than their previous participants.

"*If* you get down," I correct, setting off another round of his increasingly creative threats and my uncontrollable laughter.

The bond might be pushing me toward Windsmere, but maybe this detour wasn't such a bad idea after all.

***

"I will never forgive you for this." Milori leans heavily on his horse as we set off again for Windsmere, my stomach aching from how hard I've laughed.

"I do recall you were the one convinced this would be the perfect Human cultural experience," I say between chuckles.

"It looked a lot funnier from a distance. Ugh, I think I'm going to be sick... again." His already pale face blanches further as he heaves over the side of his mount.

"Just think—in a couple hours you'll be lounging in a fancy castle bed. Another thrilling Human experience awaiting you." I mean it as a jest, but we both know what we're riding into is far from amusing.

Chapter 11

Garrick

The towering spires of Windsmere Castle pierce the darkening sky like jagged teeth, their white stone is turned golden by the setting sun. Guards in polished armor patrol the battlements, torchlight glinting off their steel breastplates and sharp spears. The sheer scale of the fortress speaks to Human ambition—they may lack magic, but they compensate with stone and steel.

Milori transforms beside me. Gone is the ridiculous Fae who lost his lunch on a village swing. In his place sits a Day Court noble, spine straight as a sword, chin lifted with practiced arrogance. Even his voice changes, taking on that cultured accent the Fae nobles use.

"Announce us to your commanders," he calls up to the guards. "I am Ambassador Milori of the Day Court, here on official business from King Timas himself." Milori leaves no room for argument, his commanding presence would make any normal person buckle.

The guards exchange loaded glances, their eyes drawn inevitably to my massive green form like moths to flame. One grips his spear tighter, bringing his knuckles to a stark white. "And the... Orc?" The way he spits the word makes my jaw clench. I've heard worse than his tone but I know the underlying thoughts they have of my kind.

Milori's friendly demeanor vanishes. When he speaks, his voice carries the deadly edge I've seen him use in battle. "Watch your tone, Human. You may address him as Garrick, brother to Queen Emilia of the Day Court. I suggest you choose your next words with extreme caution. I'd hate to have to cut your tongue out for insulting my queen's brother."

The guard's face drains of color, a satisfying thing to watch. Several hurried whispers pass between the men before one of them goes running off to inform the king no doubt. After a few moments the massive iron-banded gates groan open with the screech of metal on metal.

The courtyard beyond speaks of wealth—marble fountains, perfectly trimmed hedges, and paths lined with expensive stone imported from the southern quarries.

Two men await us at the base of the grand stairs, and my heart pounds harder knowing Alette must have walked these same steps. My mind knows she is here and I can barely control my own legs from climbing off this horse and demanding to see her.

The older of the two carries himself like a predator. Auburn hair and sharp features enhance his grim gaze scrutinizing our every move.

Beside him stands a younger man who mirrors his stance, though something softer lingers in his eyes. I wonder if these are Alette's brothers.

"Welcome to Windsmere. I am Rowan, heir to Windsmere." Rowan's smile is all teeth and his eyes cold as winter. "To what do we owe the pleasure of a Day Court visit at this late hour?" He tries for a pleasant tone but it does not hide his annoyance that we are here.

The bond surges within me like a tide, so powerful I have to grip my reins to stay steady. She's here, somewhere in this maze of stone, she's here. The leather creaks under my fingers as Milori begins the delicate dance of diplomacy, but all I can focus on is the pull drawing me deeper into the depths of the castle.

Milori speaks with the cultured authority only a true Fae noble can manage, "While I do appreciate the customary greetings, perhaps we might continue this discussion inside? It's most unbecoming to leave King Timas' personal emissary standing in the courtyard like a common merchant." The insult is clear and does exactly what he wants it to do. And while he dons a simple mask of diplomacy, it tires and Rowan begins to see through it. A muscle twitches in the Human prince's jaw at the subtle rebuke, but he maintains his diplomatic smile. "Of course. Though I'm afraid His Majesty has retired for the evening—" The excuse is perfectly formed on his lips but Milori doesn't stand for it.

"Then he shall have to be disturbed." Milori's tone leaves no room for arguments. "I come on direct orders from King Timas himself to ensure Princess Alette's safe return after her... unfortunate experience with abduction. I'm certain your father would not want to risk offense by delaying such an important matter." The game Milori plays is one of patience, it is a good thing he is the one speaking and not me. At this point I would prefer to storm the door and find Alette now.

The bond surges at the mere thought of her name. The erratic darkness inside me simmering just at the surface. I force my breathing to remain steady, though my hands clench tighter on the reins.

"Naturally, we want to maintain good relations with the Day Court." The younger man says. This must be her younger brother, Cedric. He steps forward, something calculating in his gaze as it flicks between Milori and me. "Please, allow us to have your horses tended to while we escort you to more comfortable surroundings." He lingers on me for a moment, something in his look telling me he is playing his own game.

"Most gracious." Milori dismounts with fluid grace, every movement designed to remind them of Fae superiority without explicitly stating it. "Though I must insist on seeing the king tonight. Some matters cannot wait until morning."

I follow his lead, my bulk making several nearby guards shift nervously. My boots hit the pristine marble, dirt falling from them and I am pleased by the evidence of my presence. The brothers exchange a loaded glance before Rowan gives a curt nod and turns to head up the large stairs.

"Very well. Follow me."

The buzz of anticipation to see Alette is almost intolerable. Weeks ago, when I knew I could see her at any moment in the palace, I would feel slight jolts of excitement and connection but this, this feels like I have been starved of her presence and even one look would be enough to keep the darkness at bay.

We follow behind them at a distance and Milori drops his voice low so only I can hear him.

"I do not trust this Rowan. There is something wrong here but I just can't put my finger on it." Milori's keen eye catches things even the most adept courtier would miss. Taking his warnings to heart, I catalogue everything I can. The placement of the guards, the layout of the castle.

We are ushered into a large room with a warm blazing fire that sits in an ornate fireplace on the far wall. The furniture is expensive which isn't all that surprising but the giant paintings of, who I am assuming is the king, dominating the wall is. Not one, but three of them. His beady eyes unsettle me and the arrogance you have to have to hang a picture of yourself has stalled my mind.

"Please have a seat while I go to speak with the king." Rowan quickly glances at Cedric, an unspoken understanding passing between them, as he exits the room quickly.

After a moment Cedric walks to the door, looking outside before walking quickly back.

"Are you here to help my sister?" Cedric's entire demeanour changes. The stiff royal air he carried with his brother is gone.

Immediately I am on edge, what does Alette need help with? Milori and I look at each other, both of us concerned.

"Is Alette in danger?" my voice rumbles as the bond flares and my deep desire to protect my soul bond consumes me. Cedric takes a step back, surprised by the anger in my voice. I try to calm myself but struggle to do so. Milori steps forward, seeing the war raging inside of me and the fear on Cedric's face.

"Now, listen to me carefully, Cedric. I don't want to have to hurt my friend here to protect you, so I need you to answer my questions quickly and to the point." Milori's calm voice seems to put Cedric at ease, at least for a moment, until he looks at me again.

I can feel my body shaking, trying to hold myself back from slamming this puny boy against the wall and beating him until he tells me exactly where my Alette is.

"Is Alette here and safe?" Milori asks Cedric.

As instructed, he answers quickly and to the point, "Yes, she is in her bedchambers, safe with her lady's maid, Corrine." A bit of my inner tension breaks, letting me breathe a little better.

"Good, good, that's good." Milori takes another step forward, working himself between me and the Human. The rage that simmers is still a flame, but I won't be satisfied until I can see her and know she is safe.

Cedric's eyes bounce between Milori and me, and I know he is trying to figure out what is going on. To any normal person, they might just think I have gone insane. That assessment isn't far from the truth.

"What is wrong with him?" Cedric whispers, as if I can't hear him. But all my energy is focused on not destroying everything in this room. My soul bond is in danger, and I was an idiot for fighting the bond.

"Well, that's a particularly interesting story, but suffice it to say that this big green guy behind me is your sister's soul bond. Right now, you have told him she is in danger, and of what we do not know. Now, my big green friend has been trying to ignore this bond for too long. With Orcs, well, when they ignore the soul bond, they go a little insane if they don't act on it." Milori sums up my situation so perfectly, it's hard to hear. I put myself in this situation, and instead of telling Alette how I feel and what I feared, I tried to run and ignore it.

"My sister has a soul bond... to an Orc?" He doesn't sound disgusted but he is certainly surprised. Noise comes from the hall and any confusion is tossed aside as he seems to pull himself together.

"Alright, my father is coming but he will not let you see my sister, not tonight or ever if he can manage. I promise you she is safe but she does need allies." He uses the word carefully, likely trying to avoid me getting more 'whatever I am' right now. "But I will bring her to you later when you have been set up in your rooms."

The door to the room opens and in walks Rowan, along with an older version of himself. The resemblance is striking whereas Cedric looks more like Alette with his dark blonde hair.

Milori seamlessly slips back into his role while maintaining his presence in front of me. With everything I am, I urge my body to relax. *She's here and she's safe.* I repeat it over and over again until I feel the muscles release. My growing headache from straining slows to a halt.

"What a surprise," comes from the older king. He walks in with all the authority he can possess, but even in comparison to Milori, he does not command the same space. "I was not informed an emissary was en route; had I known, I would have made better accommodations for your arrival." I can practically smell the lie he spews, but I try not to react.

"I'm sure you would have, but this way, we can see what the Human kingdom is truly able to accomplish. Besides, King Timas is never required to inform anyone he is sending an emissary or showing up himself." The threat of Timas showing up seems to unsettle the king, which brings me far too much joy.

"Well, I would prefer advance notice, if the king of the Day Court would be so kind next time." The king gives a tight smile but pushes on. "I am sorry, but you will not be able to meet with Alette tonight. I am unsure of your Fae customs, but here, the princess is not to be seen after a certain hour, and it has passed. I assure you we are grateful for what Timas—"

"King Timas," Milori corrects him, and the muscle in his jaw ticks with anger.

"King Timas has done for the princess. You are welcome to join us in the morning for breakfast, where you will be able to see her. Now, I have had several rooms prepared for you. I trust you will find the accommodations adequate." The king finally looks at me before focusing his attention back on Milori. "And though your guest is the brother of the queen, may I remind you that many are not hospitable to Orcs here, especially since a bunch of battle-crazy Orcs stole her away from us. Now, if you'll excuse me." The king turns on his heel and stomps out of the room. Rowan follows suit, leaving us alone with Cedric once more.

My presence obviously upsets him, but no part of me cares that he has such disdain for me. My concern is for Alette. The way he spoke of her does not shout loving daughter but rather an instrument of the crown.

What has my soul bond been through? Just another thing to regret.

Cedric leads down the large halls, only the sound of our shoes scuffing the floor for noise. The castle is deathly quiet, the entire place feels as if it has no life at all.

Finally getting to a long corridor with two doors on either side Cedric turns to us.

"These are your rooms, yours on the left," he points to me, "and yours on the right. I beg your pardon, but I did not ask for your names." He seems to have recovered from my display and is composing himself well– how admirable.

"Milori, and this is Garrick. Alette will be pleased to know he's here." Milori's comment is just a way for him to antagonize me but the thought that I will get to see her soon practically lights me on fire.

"I will bring her to your room, Garrick. There is a secret passage that sits to the left of the fireplace, do not be alarmed when it moves." Cedric, whatever his intentions, seems to be in support of Alette. Mustering everything I can, I try to keep my voice level when I speak to him.

"Thank you." The strain is evident but I see sympathy in his eyes, and regret, but I don't know why.

Cedric heads back the way we came while Milori sighs loudly.

"Well, this has been quite the day. Alright, big guy, let's go wait for your soul bond." He slaps me on the shoulder and I grunt in agreement. "I hope this doesn't blow up in our faces," he mutters as he opens up my room door.

You and me both, Milori.

Chapter 12

Alette

The soft glow of the lantern casts shadows on the floor, its flickering flame my only distraction as sleep eludes me. Pushing the heavy blankets off, I sit up and swing my feet out of bed, the soft rug barely registering with the turmoil inside me.

I can't stop thinking about Garrick. It has become an incessant and persistent thought, and no matter how hard I try to push him away, it won't go. Emotion builds pressure in my throat and behind my eyes. A knock at my door startles me.

"Princess?" Corrine's voice is barely above a whisper.

"Come in." I hastily wipe my eyes as she slips inside, her face drawn with worry.

"The guards are all stirred up. Apparently some Fae noble arrived tonight—with an Orc." My heart skips at her words, but I force my face to remain neutral. "They've doubled the patrols, especially near your wing. Your father seems... unsettled by their presence. I thought you should know, in case you wondered why there was so much foot traffic outside your door." Her thoughtful consideration warms my heart and I try to force a smile in gratitude.

"Thank you, Corrine, for informing me. You may go," I whisper. She hesitates for a moment, unsure if she should stay or go, but eventually moves towards the door despite her reservations.

After Corrine leaves, I curl up on my bed, wrapping my arms around my knees. Though it is a surprise there is a Fae noble here, my mind goes back to my previous thoughts.

How can a man have such a hold on me? Even the letters would be better to dwell on, though they too battle for attention in my mind. The words and kindness were so tender and soft, and it all feels so unfair.

I cry softly into my knees. The sadness of my arranged marriage, the reality of my future, and the desire for a man who wanted nothing to do with me... Maybe, just for now, I will let it all out so that tomorrow I can pick up the pieces and face my future.

The sound of stone scraping stone draws my attention, halting my tears. My heart races as I watch the old passageway beside my bookshelf begin to open. Few know of these passages—who would dare use them tonight with extra guards about?

Cedric's face appears in the dim firelight, eyes wide with urgency. Of course it's him. I showed him those passages when we were young, a fun way to play in the castle without having to worry about the guards reporting our every move to Father.

Before he can speak, footsteps echo down the corridor outside my door. Several guards moving quickly and with purpose.

"Get in bed!" he mouths, disappearing back into the passage.

The wall slides shut just as my door handle turns. My heart thuds wildly in my chest as I dive under the covers, attempting to slow my breathing as my door opens. Rowan's figure enters my room, the light from the hall shining behind him. He strides inside with purpose, scanning the entire room. Through barely-closed eyes, I watch him prowl around my chambers, checking behind curtains and in corners. His sharp gaze lingers on the bookshelf before he finally leaves, the door clicking shut behind him.

I count to one hundred and wait, listening intently for any more movement from outside my door but I don't hear anything. While my heart pumps fiercely in my chest, I slip out of bed and make my way over to the passage door. The passage creaks open again and Cedric's face reappears.

"That was too close," he whispers. "Are you alright?"

"What are you doing here?" I whisper back, though there's no real need. I'm alone in my chambers, and the door is locked—no one is coming in without permission now that Rowan has done his inspection.

I move closer, and Cedric can see I've been crying. Immediately he comes forward to gently grab my hands, concern etched on his face.

"What's the matter? What happened?" The change in Cedric has been amazing, but it is still strange to have someone care so much... at all.

"Oh, it's nothing. Just thinking." I hastily wipe away the tears in hopes that I will look better, though I know it won't really help. They are likely red from crying and no amount of rubbing is going to make it better.

"Well, maybe I can put a smile on your face." He says hopefully, though his eyes keep darting to the door as if expecting Rowan to return.

"How are you going to do that? Is my betrothal cancelled?" The sadness in his face reveals that it's not the surprise he has for me.

"No," he winces at his own answer. "But I have someone here you might want to see." I raise a brow in question. Who could possibly be here? I just sent some letters today. I doubt they have reached their destination. A brief thought goes to the guests that have arrived unexpectedly, but I push it out of my mind. "Come on." He pulls me towards the secret passageway.

"Wait— let me get my robe." I rush to grab the delicate garment. It does little more than cover my nightgown, but it's comforting.

He grins from ear to ear and it actually makes me feel happier despite my earlier sadness. A mix of fear and excitement flutters in my stomach at the sight, one thing is for sure though, I do trust Cedric. He takes my hand, raising a lantern with his other. The flickering light casts eerie shadows as we move deeper into the passages. Every creak of stone, every distant echo makes my heart jump. What if Rowan followed us somehow?

"How do you know where we're going?" I whisper as he takes a sharp right down a passage I've never seen. These tunnels feel endless, like a maze designed to trap unwary wanderers.

A sound from above makes us both freeze. Footsteps, moving across the floor overhead. We press against the cold stone wall, barely breathing as they pass. I can't imagine they would be able to hear us, but whatever is happening in the castle right now is making it very difficult to move around freely.

"How do you think I spent my time after I came here?" Cedric finally answers, his voice tight. "Certainly wasn't playing with Rowan." The bitterness in his words breaks my heart. While I had Gardenia Manor as a refuge from Father's demands, Cedric had only these dark passages.

We continue on, each step feeling both too fast and too slow. My mind races with possibilities. Who could be so important that Cedric would risk sneaking me through the castle at night?

Finally, we stop before another door. The excitement radiating from Cedric is palpable, but something else thrums in the air. An inexplicable pull, like a thread tugging at my very soul.

"Ready?" Cedric asks, setting down the lantern. His hands shake slightly as he pushes against the wall.

I nod, though my heart pounds so hard I fear it might burst. The stone scrapes open, revealing warm firelight beyond. Cedric takes my hand again, steadying me as I step through.

Nothing could have prepared me for what—who—awaits on the other side.

We walk into a beautiful room, perfectly decorated but that's not what makes me lose my breath–it's the two men in the room that brings a whole flood of fresh tears to my eyes.

"Why is she crying?" Garrick's voice cascades over me, a feeling of comfort and safety that I both love and hate. Is this a nightmare, to show me what I will never have? I fall to my knees and bury my face in my hands.

"I don't know. She was crying when I found her in her room but she was happy by the time we got here. You said you were her soul bond. Shouldn't she be happy to see you?"

Cedric's words float in the back of my mind as I become overwhelmed with emotion. The recognition of the words 'soul bond' dance in my mind but I am so overcome with sadness that I just can't think. In my tear-filled state I didn't realize that someone had come to kneel in front of me. A large hand gently touches mine and that familiar spark dances up my arm at the touch. Gently, so gently, he pulls my hands from my face and with his big palm he tilts my face up to see his.

The man I have dreamt about, and hoped to glimpse, kneels in front of me. His blue eyes, my own personal pool to fall into. Everything around us stops and all I can feel is his presence.

"I don't understand." I barely manage to say.

"I'm sorry." Garrick's voice is rough and his eyes mist with his own tears. I find myself so confused at what is happening.

"Why are you here?" The question sits heavy on us, I know the answer to it is going to change everything.

"For you. I'm here for you." A wave of shock, confusion, and elation wash over me, leaving me breathless and wondering if this moment was truly happening.

"But you hate me." I hear a shocked expression from behind the giant man in front of me. I hate how vulnerable I sound, but at this point I don't have anything left to protect myself. My emotions are drained and I just don't have it in me to pretend like I normally do. Garrick rubs his thumb over my cheek, the motion bringing a deep bone comfort I didn't know even existed.

"I don't hate you, Alette. What I feel for you is the opposite of what I've shown to you." He takes a deep breath in before continuing. "You, my little ember, are everything. You are my soul bond."

I suck in a breath at the name. My little ember.

"It's you?" The letters I received in Sonas, the beautiful words that brought me so much comfort and joy.

He nods, but shame still covers his face. "I am a coward." His voice comes out rough with emotion. His large hands cradle my face with a gentleness that makes my heart ache. "When I first saw you, sitting there on that walkway in the depths of the shrouded forest, I thought I was dreaming. Your beauty captivated me and my soul cried out for yours... But I was afraid." His blue eyes shimmer with unshed tears, the vulnerability in them taking my breath away. "Instead of having the courage to face what I felt, I ran. I made you feel like you were nothing to me when you're everything. I will never forgive myself for how I treated you."

His thumb catches another tear as it falls down my cheek, the touch sending sparks of warmth through my entire body.

"Those letters–every word was true, Little Ember. You consumed my thoughts until I could barely breathe. The bond between us..." His voice breaks, and I feel his hands tremble against my skin. "I'm here now because I couldn't bear another day without telling you the truth. You're my soul bond, the other half of my very being. I understand if you want me to leave and never return, but I had to tell you– Had to let you know that everything I wrote, everything I feel for you, is real."

The truth of his words washes over me like a wave, threatening to pull me under. Garrick–the letters were from Garrick. While I was mourning the loss of my secret admirer, believing I would never read those beautiful words again, it was him all along. The same man who could barely look at me, who turned away whenever I entered a room, had been writing me those tender, soul-touching letters.

"The tea..." My voice comes out small and broken. The memory of that earthy blend, how it had brought me comfort when everything else felt cold and hopeless, takes on new meaning. Another gift from him, when I thought he hated me.

"I saw you in the garden that day." His deep voice rumbles through me, those strong hands still impossibly gentle against my tear-stained cheeks. "You looked so sad, and I... I couldn't bear it. Even if I was too much of a coward to face you properly."

Something pulls at my chest, an invisible thread drawing me closer to him. Is this what he means by soul bond? All those times my heart would flutter wildly at his presence in Sonas, how I kept finding excuses to walk past the forge–it wasn't just my foolish heart betraying me. There was something deeper, something real.

"I felt something too." The words tumble out before I can stop them, very unprincess-like in their desperation. "Every time you were near, it was like... like being pulled toward warmth on a cold day. I thought I was going mad, wanting someone who couldn't stand the sight of me."

His massive frame shudders at my words. "Little Ember..." The nickname from his letters makes fresh tears spill down my cheeks. "I'll spend the rest of my days making up for how I hurt you."

The rest of his days. Reality crashes back like one of Father's cruel lectures. "Garrick, the engagement ball is tomorrow..." My voice catches as fear claws at my throat. "If Father finds you here, he'll-"

"Let me worry about your father," he growls, the sound sending an entirely inappropriate shiver down my spine. Even now, with everything crumbling around me, his presence makes me feel safer than I have in years.

"You don't understand." My fingers clutch at his shirt, the fabric rough against my skin. "Father will never allow this. Bertram Blackthorn's dowry is too valuable, the alliance too important." The words taste like ash in my mouth, the familiar cage of duty closing in.

"We'll find a way." His blue eyes burn with determination, and for a moment I let myself believe him. "I won't lose you again, Little Ember. Not to him, not to anyone."

I should pull away. Should remember my place, my duty, everything I've been trained since birth to be. But here in this secret room, with Garrick's warmth surrounding me and that strange golden thread pulling us together, I can't bring myself to move. For once in my life, I feel... whole.

A noise from behind Garrick reminds me we aren't alone and immediately my cheeks heat from embarrassment.

"Oh, don't mind us," Milori says with his usual dramatic flair. "Just enjoying the show. Though I must say, you're much more articulate than I expected, you green giant." I can hear the teasing tone in his voice but I am more embarrassed that they saw this entire exchange.

Garrick growls but doesn't move from his position in front of me. If anything, he shifts slightly to block me more from view, though his touch remains gentle. I lean forward placing my head on his chest, thoroughly mortified.

"And letters! I didn't know you even knew how to write!" Milori continues teasing him and I can't help the laugh that escapes me, which seems to ease some tension in Garrick.

"Enough, Milori." There is no bite to his words as Garrick threatens, " And if you breathe a word of this to Emilia..."

"Oh, I'm telling her everything," Milori declares with obvious glee. "Especially the part where you nicknamed your soul bond, what is it now? 'Little Ember'? Emilia is going to love that, especially since you made fun of Timas' pet name for her." Milori is having far too much fun. I lean back again, a smile stretching across my face to see an annoyed Garrick in front of me.

"Milori," Garrick warns, but I feel his own embarrassment in the way his hands tremble slightly against my skin.

"As touching as this is," Cedric interrupts, his voice taking on an edge of urgency, "Alette needs to return to her room. Rowan may have checked on her once but who's to say he won't do it again."

"Cedric's right," I murmur. Garrick's hands tighten slightly around mine. I look up at him, my voice wavering, "You'll come back?" I ask barely above a whisper. "What does this mean—this soul bond?"

"I know there is so much I need to explain but it will have to wait until tomorrow," he murmurs, his thumb brushing my cheek one last time. "At breakfast, I'll be there as part of Milori's guard detail. We can't show any recognition, but I'll be there."

"We all play our parts," Milori adds, his usual playful tone replaced with something more serious. "The arrogant Fae noble and his brooding Orc companion come to ensure the princess' safe return. No one will suspect anything more."

Cedric shifts nervously by the passage entrance. "We need to go, Alette. Now."

My heart aches as I pull away from Garrick's warmth. So many questions burn on my tongue—about the letters, the bond, everything... but they'll have to wait. The reality of my position, of tomorrow's engagement ball, settles back over me like a heavy cloak.

"Be safe, Little Ember," Garrick says softly as I turn to follow Cedric.

The journey back through the passages feels longer somehow, each step taking me further from answers I desperately want. But, at least now, I know. The letters, the tea, the feeling of being watched with tenderness rather than judgment—it was all real. Whatever tomorrow brings, I'm no longer alone.

Chapter 13

Garrick

Can't sleep. Can't think. Can't do anything but pace this oversized room like some caged beast. The bond burns under my skin, darker and more demanding than ever. Now that I've stopped fighting it, the pull to find Alette is nearly unbearable.

My hands shake as I make another circuit of the room. The memory of her tears last night tears at my gut. She thought I hated her. Goddess, what kind of monster am I?

"By the sun, you're going to wear through their precious marble if you keep that up." Milori sprawls in one of those fancy chairs they gave us, looking annoyingly comfortable. "Though that might actually improve this place. Humans have no taste."

I grunt, not breaking stride. Dawn's light is barely touching the windows but I've been up for hours, fighting the urge to tear through this castle until I find her.

"We need to tell him." The words claw their way out before I can stop them.

Milori raises an eyebrow at me. "Tell who what?"

"The king, about the bond." My fists clench as another wave of darkness rolls through me. "He's her father. Maybe if he understands—"

"Are you actually insane?" Milori's usual smirk vanishes. He stands, suddenly every bit the king's captain. "Have those muscles finally crushed what little brains you have left?"

"Then what's your brilliant plan, pretty boy?" The darkness surges, making my voice come out as more of a growl. "Stand around while she marries that pathetic son of a duke?" I throw my hands up in frustration. I need to get myself under control.

"My plan is to keep you alive long enough to actually help her." He plants himself in my path, forcing me to stop. "Think about it, Garrick. That man barely tolerates you being here as the queen's brother. How do you think he'll react when he finds out his precious daughter—who I am fairly certain he actually doesn't care about—is soul-bonded to a half-breed?"

The words hit as hard as a physical blow, all of my fears and concerns brought to light—but he's not wrong. Doesn't make the rage any easier to swallow though.

"I won't let her marry him." The darkness in my blood makes the words come out deadly quiet.

"No, you won't." For once there's no mockery in Milori's voice. "But if you go charging in there announcing yourself as her soul bond, best case is you end up in chains. Worst case?" He lets out a heavy breath. "They'll kill you and force her to marry him anyway."

The bond surges at the thought, making me grip the back of a chair so hard the wood breaks. "There has to be—"

A knock cuts me off. Both Milori and I stare at the door.

"Don't break anything else," Milori chastises as he goes to the door. I release my hold on the chair, stretching out my hand to try and release the tension.

"His Majesty requests your presence for breakfast." The voice is muffled by the door and space and I take deep breaths to calm the raging storm inside me.

I take strong deliberate steps toward the door clinging to what little control I have over my body. The servant visibly shakes when he sees me. That dark part inside me is happy by his reaction; let them be afraid.

"We would be *delighted*." Milori's court mask slides back into place, all fake smiles and fancy manners. The servant spins on his heel and heads down the hall, practically running. A smile nearly emerges on my face.

Milori turns to me before following after the servant. "You need to maintain control. Play your part. We will come up with a way to get her out of this but if you explode at breakfast there will be no rescuing her and there will be no bond." He emphasises his last few words making it abundantly clear what I have to do.

The thought of never truly being with Alette is enough to push the rage away but I don't know for how long. I nod grimly. Play the surly guard and brother to the queen? Pretend I barely notice her? Every part of me rebels against the idea, but he's right. One wrong look and it all falls apart.

"Ready to face the wolves, you great green lump?" The familiar insult actually helps the turmoil swirling around inside me. A bit of normalcy to weather this storm. It almost makes me smile. Almost.

"Just try not to trip over those fancy boots, dancing fairy," I naturally quip back. Yet no matter how sharp our words, I know he always has my best interests at heart. He'll do everything he can to help Alette—I'm certain of that.

The castle feels unnaturally quiet for a place full of nobles preparing for an upcoming party. The halls are sparse, the stillness broken only by the guards stationed every few meters—a thin facade of strength the king clings to.

Rounding the corner, I come face to face with a massive set of doors leading into the dining hall. I pause, taking one last steadying breath, bracing myself against the bond's relentless pull. Alette is waiting inside. Whatever happens next, I won't fail her again.

The doors open to a room dripping with gaudy wealth. Massive portraits of the king cover nearly every wall—as if one wasn't enough to show his arrogance. The long table gleams with gold and silver, every piece placed to scream power and control.

Then I see her, and everything else fades away.

Alette sits rigidly in her chair, wearing a pale pink dress that makes her look washed out and small. Cedric sits on her right, a physical barrier between her, the king and heir.

She is a shell of a person, nothing like the vibrant woman I saw in Sonas. Her face is a perfect mask of polite attention, but I see the way her fingers grip her dress too tight–that slight tremor in her hand as she lifts her cup.

Bertram lounges across from her like he owns the place, his eyes roving over her in a way that makes the bond howl for violence. My hands shake with the need to tear him apart. *No, I need to focus. I can't help her if I am locked away.*

"You must be famished after your journey." The king's voice scrapes against my nerves. Rowan watches us enter, scrutinizing us with every step.

"Though I confess, I'm surprised King Timas sent such an... interesting delegation." The king's eyes linger on my green skin with barely concealed disgust.

Taking our seats near the end, Milori turns his razor sharp eyes towards the king. The man to his right has barely looked up from his plate, completely bored by the interaction.

"Interesting?" Milori's voice carries a deadly edge. "You mean the brother of Queen Emilia, wife to the most powerful Fae in existence?" His cultured tone drips with venom. "Though I suppose someone so... provincial might struggle to comprehend why King Timas values strength of character over appearances. The Day Court has evolved beyond such petty prejudices."

I focus on my breathing and on not crushing the delicate chair they've given me. Even though Milori's defense of me sparks a pride within that I can't ignore, the bond still pulses angrily beneath my skin at the king's obvious disdain.

Bertram leans across the table to Alette, speaking just loud enough to carry.

"You look especially lovely this morning, my dear," Bertram says smoothly, his hand reaching out to touch hers where it rests on her glass. She pulls back quickly, avoiding his touch; the movement subtle but noticed by everyone at the table. The slight against Bertram sparks far more satisfaction in me than it should.

"I do hope you're looking forward to our dance tonight," he continues, his tone deceptively sweet but laced with quiet menace. "I've been practicing specifically for you." His words might seem charming, but the undercurrent of his tone reveals the insult has not gone unnoticed. He won't let it pass—his kind never does.

A surge of anger prickles across my skin. The fork in my hand bends under the pressure of my grip. Milori kicks me under the table, a silent warning to keep my temper in check.

"Tell me, Your Majesty," Milori smoothly interjects, "I heard whispers of rebel Fae causing trouble along your borders. Quite concerning."

The king's face darkens. "Indeed. Though perhaps if the Day Court had better control over its subjects..."

"Or perhaps if certain kingdoms didn't levy impossible taxes on their farmers, leaving them vulnerable to raiders." The words slip out of my mouth before I can stop them. Every head at the table turns to me—some faces a mix of shock, while others seething with anger.

Alette's eyes widen slightly, the first real spark of emotion I've seen from her all day. The king turns an impressive shade of purple, and I savor it more than I should.

"You dare—" he starts, but Milori cuts him off with a smooth, disarming laugh.

"My companion has spent much time among the common folk. He often forgets his place." Milori's tone is light, but his words carry a warning. *Focus, Garrick.* "Though I'm certain Your Majesty has the situation well in hand," he adds, twisting the knife into the king's already wounded pride.

"Of course he does," Bertram interjects, his voice a syrupy blend of charm and condescension. His gaze slides toward Alette, a thin veneer of civility failing to hide the possessiveness in his eyes. "Just as I'll have everything well in hand once the princess and I are married. Women need a firm, guiding hand to show them their place, wouldn't you agree?"

The darkness surges through my blood like wildfire. The chair arm splinters in my grip. Alette's face stays carefully blank but I see her shoulders tense, see the way she seems to fold in on herself.

"I've always found that the truly powerful need not speak of their power." Milori's words cut like a knife. "Those who do, tend to be... compensating for something."

Bertram flushes angrily but whatever response he might have made is cut off by servants bringing in more food. The interruption is enough to halt the conversation, which is probably for the best. I'm not sure how much more I could have taken of it. To keep up appearances, I eat but the food tastes bland and forgettable; I am too focused on staying calm to notice any of it.

This is what her life has been like–what it will continue to be like if I don't find a way to save her. My heart breaks for my soul bond, to live in such a suffocating place, unable to be her true self must be a nightmare. The bond pulses with fierce protective fury as I watch her endure their casual cruelty with practiced grace.

I catch Milori's eye and see my own anger reflected there. He is just as shocked as I am to see the king's court. I thought the Orc's were a harsh race but I was wrong; Humans are far worse, and they lack respect.

After the torturous breakfast finally ends, I pull Milori aside in the corridor. "I need to see her. Before the ball." I'm not ashamed of the pleading tone, she is my everything and I won't fall back into my weak ways of running.

"Are you trying to get us both executed?" But there's less bite in his words than usual. He witnessed the same treatment as I saw.

"Please." The word feels strange in my mouth but I'm desperate enough to beg. "There are things she needs to know about the bond. Things I should have told her last night." Besides the fact I just need to see her... to touch her. To remind myself she is real and safe.

Milori studies me for a long moment before sighing dramatically. "Fine. But only because you said please." He smirks. "Thought I'd never hear that word from your brutish mouth."

Cedric appears from around the corner. Milori and I exchange a glance—*that could have been anyone.* I need to watch where I'm talking.

"The eastern garden should be empty at this time of day. I'll bring her there in an hour," Cedric says before walking away with the practiced stride of a stuck-up noble. Still, I've seen the way he tries to make his sister happy. I don't know what their relationship is really like, but everything he does feels like he's trying to atone for something. Strange.

Chapter 14

Garrick

An hour feels like an eternity. The bond pulses beneath my skin with an almost unbearable urgency. How Timas endured waiting to be with Emilia, I'll never understand. This desire burns through me; a primal call that consumes every thought, every breath.

The garden, when I find it, is a poor imitation of the ones in Sonas. Everything is too rigid, too controlled. But even this garden, and the ones in Sonas, are nothing compared to the rugged beauty of the Southern mountains, with their wild spaces and untamed wildflowers. One day I will take Alette there, if she'll allow me. But for now this will have to do, it's private and that's what we need.

I wander over to the large fountain at the center of the garden, where a statue of a woman appears to dance gracefully as water cascades around her like rain. It's oddly happy compared to the polished look of the rest of the castle.

I hear her before I see her, the bond humming to life at her presence. She appears through an archway of perfectly trimmed roses, Cedric hovering protectively nearby.

"I'll keep watch," he says, giving Alette a small smile before turning to leave us alone.

Alette stands by the archway, uncertain for a moment before something in her face shifts into determination and she closes the distance between us. Without the audience from last night, or this morning, I can finally look at her properly. Truly see her.

"You look tired, Little Ember." The words slip out before I can stop them. Dark circles shadow her hazel eyes, barely hidden by whatever paints they use here. Her stress-ridden shoulders are pulled tight from the face she puts on.

"I couldn't sleep." She wrings her hands together, a nervous gesture I've never seen from her in Sonas. "I kept thinking... wondering if it was all a dream." She looks up at me, still unsure if it was a dream.

The vulnerability in her voice makes my chest ache. My feet have a mind of their own and immediately moves closer to her. I reach for her hands and she willingly– excitedly–grabs them in return. The contact sends warmth racing up my arms, the bond singing between us.

"Not a dream." My voice comes out rough. "Though I don't deserve your trust after how I treated you." Shame nearly suffocates me. "You deserve better than me." The truth weighs down on us but I don't see contempt in her eyes, just acceptance.

"I think... I think I deserve happiness and you make me happy." Something inside of me roars in triumph. Pulling her hands to my chest I lean my forehead down to hers. She smells perfect, of fresh air and mountain rains. She is everything.

"Tell me about the bond?" She pulls back to look up at me with those beautiful hazel eyes. "I feel... something. Like being pulled toward warmth on a cold day. Is that normal?"

I guide her to a stone bench, keeping her hands in mine. The touch grounds me, keeping the darkness at bay. These moments, I am realizing, are the only time I can have complete control of myself.

"Both the Fae and Orcs have bonds, but they work differently. For Orcs, the goddess gifts us—if we are lucky—one perfect match. The elders say soul bonds strengthen our people and the children born from them carry that strength." I can't help but smile when Alette's cheeks turn pink at the mention of children. "These bonds are sacred—a gift from the gods that connects two people so deeply that nothing can break them apart. They complete each other in every way."

I pause, knowing the next part is harder to explain. "But soul bonds aren't like spirit bonds. When an Orc finds their soul bond, it hits instantly and we have to act on it right away." My throat tightens as I force out the next words. "If we don't..." I squeeze her hands gently, hating this part. "The Orc loses themselves. All control, all civility just... disappears. We become the monsters everyone already thinks we are." The shame of my earlier actions weighs heavy as I tell her this.

"Were you fighting the bond? Is that why you were avoiding me?" I can hear the pain in her voice and I wish I could take it away—but I am the one who put it there.

"Yes." Shame burns in my gut. "I was a coward. I was afraid–I was afraid you would take one look at me and leave like my mother did." The pain of abandonment hasn't left me, even at my age. "I convinced myself I wasn't worthy of you. That you deserved better than a half-breed blacksmith. But all I did was hurt us both..."

Her fingers tighten around mine. "You're not the only one who's afraid." Her voice barely rises above a whisper. "Everything I am has been shaped by others. Every choice being made for me–even this..." She gestures to her pink dress, frustration evident in the sharp movement. "Father picks the colours I wear, the words I speak. Every detail of my life, controlled." The meek woman who sat in the dining hall this morning vanishes, replaced by the Alette I watched from afar. That fire in her eyes urges my heart to soar.

"You chose for me, too... just like everyone else. I'm afraid of all this—whatever this is—but I had a right to choose for myself. For once in my life, I want to make that decision. You don't get to make this one for me." Her chest heaves with emotion, and despite the sting of her words, I am beyond proud to see her fight for herself, even if I am one of the many who have taken her rights away.

"You're right." I run my thumb over her knuckles. "You deserve to choose. Even now, you can tell me to leave and I will go. I will never bother you again if that would make you happy. But in all my stupidity, I came here to tell you that if you wanted to take a chance on an idiotic Orc–who has much to learn about

wooing his soul bond–I am here, ready to give you all of me."
I pour everything I have into my words, hoping she hears me...
and believes me.

"How do I know what I am feeling is real? That I'm not
just completely enthralled with your muscles or your beautiful
skin." She reaches up and gently touches my exposed chest. A
satisfied rumble vibrates from within me, happy for her touch.

"Because the bond doesn't lie." I lift one hand to cup her
cheek, my rough palm against her soft skin. "It's not about control, or power, or politics. It's about choice. Two souls choosing
each other above all else. This is your choice, Alette."

A single tear slips down her cheek. I catch it with my thumb.
"What happens if I can't get out of all this? The betrothal... this
castle. What happens if we have to ignore it?"

"I won't let that happen, if that's your choice." The words
come out fiercer than intended. "I know I have no right to ask
you anything after what I put you through, but trust me in this,
Little Ember. I'll find a way to free you from this cage."

She leans into my touch, her eyes closing. "I'm so tired of
being afraid." When she opens them again, that spark of determination I've come to cherish burns bright. "And I choose you,
Garrick. Even though you were monumentally stupid about all
of this."

I can't help but laugh, my heart nearly bursting at her words.
"I'll spend the rest of my days making it up to you. More tea
blends, more letters—whatever you want, Little Ember."

"Whatever I want?" A small smile plays on her lips. "That's quite the promise."

"I mean it." My thumb traces her cheekbone, memorizing the softness of her skin. The bond hums between us, a golden thread pulling us closer. "May I... may I kiss you?"

Her eyes shine with tears again, but this time I see joy in them. "Yes."

I lean closer, sliding my hand down to her neck. Her breaths come short and quick, anticipation radiating from her. Her lips are a breath away, her hazel eyes shining before they flutter closed. I follow, letting my own eyes close as our lips finally meet.

She is soft where I am rough, delicate where I am strong. When she makes a quiet sound against my mouth, my grip tightens instinctively, drawing her closer as I deepen the kiss. Even the touch of my tusks do not repulse her but cause a soft sound to escape her instead.

The bond surges with protective fury at her closeness, demanding more. Her hands grip my shirt, pulling herself closer as if she feels the same desperate need. Everything about her calls to me—her warmth, her scent, the way she trembles slightly under my touch. I want to gather her in my arms, shield her from everything that's hurt her.

But footsteps approaching force us apart, both of us breathing heavily. The bond screams in protest at the separation.

"Someone's coming," Cedric hisses from his post.

Alette stands quickly, smoothing her skirts. "I should go. There's so much to prepare for tonight..."

"I'll be there." I resist the urge to pull her back to me. "Whatever happens, remember you're not alone anymore."

She nods once, giving me the sweetest smile before hurrying away with Cedric. The bond aches at her departure, but something has shifted between us.

Something needs to change and if I can't figure out what to do tonight then I may lose her forever.

Chapter 15

Alette

"Are you certain about this dress, Princess?" Corrine's fingers pause as she laces up the back of the gown, concern evident in her voice. "Your father specifically requested you wear the pink silk he had made for tonight."

She looks past me and I meet her eyes in the mirror. I love the dark green fabric, the soft elegant material wrapping around me is far more comfortable than what I usually wear. It shimmers in the late afternoon light and the silver accents catch on the sun making the stars shine.

"I am."

For once, my voice holds no trace of uncertainty because this is my choice. Father will be furious, of course he will. The dress is far too bold, too different from the ridiculous pastels he prefers. But something has shifted inside me since this morning... since Garrick. Knowing he cares for me gives me a confidence I didn't know I had.

For so many years I have fought my own battles, alone. I didn't realize with the right person at your side you feel like you can face the world with renewed confidence. Not because you didn't have it, but because they helped uncover it.

My fingers drift to my lips, remembering the gentle press of his kiss. Heat rises to my cheeks, the memory of him being so close takes my breath away. Even now, hours later, I can feel the ghost of his touch, the way something inside of me just hummed at his nearness. The bond, I suppose.

"You look beautiful." Corrine's voice softens as she secures the last lace. "Though I worry..." She doesn't finish the thought, but she doesn't need to. We both know what wearing this dress means—open defiance of Father's wishes. Excitement is mixed with fear but it feels good to finally take a stand. Garrick will be there and... well, I want to wear this for him.

"I know." I smooth my hands over the fabric, relishing its otherworldly softness. "But I'm tired of being afraid."

The words echo what I told Garrick in the garden. Looking at my reflection, I barely recognize myself. The woman staring back seems stronger—somehow more vibrant. I still bear the dark circles under my eyes since no amount of makeup can cover it, but I've changed, and this time I am choosing for me... for what I want to do.

The deep green makes my skin glow and brings out flecks of gold in my eyes. I had hoped Garrick would see the dress at the Night of the Golden Trail... at least tonight he will.

"At least let me add these." Corrine produces a delicate silver necklace with matching earrings—pieces Mother gave me years ago. My heart aches at not having seen my mother yet. I wonder if she is doing well, or whether anyone told her I was back at the castle. I should ask Cedric. "If you're going to cause a stir, you might as well do it properly." I chuckle at her comment, she is a great supporter in a world of enemies.

A knock at the door makes us both jump. I look at her confused, no one should be here yet. Cedric said he would come later to pick me up.

Corrine hurries over to the door to answer it while I finish securing the earrings with trembling fingers.

"Lord Bertram requests a moment with the princess." The servant's voice carries across the room, making my stomach clench. Bertram, already trying to assert his claim. My neck prickles with nervousness.

"Tell him the princess is not yet ready to receive visitors." Corrine's tone leaves no room for argument and I let out an exhale as she closes the door. After it clicks shut I can see her shake her head, which makes me happy. She steps up to my side and squeezes my arm lovingly before adding a few more pins to my hair.

"Thank you." The words come out shaky. Even the thought of being alone with him makes my skin crawl. I don't know how I will manage tonight but Garrick will be there and that makes me feel a little bit better.

"Always, Princess." She smiles kindly and continues with my hair. "Though you should prepare yourself. The entire court will be watching tonight." She doesn't say it in a chastising way, but in a way that warns of the vultures excited for their next meal.

"Let them watch." I lift my chin in defiance while straightening my shoulders. "I am not their puppet anymore." The words bolster my growing determination. But even as I say the words, fear coils in my stomach. The engagement ball is to announce to the court our formal intention of marrying. I don't know how I will get out of this marriage but if Garrick and Milori are willing to help I will trust that they will come up with a solution, though I can't imagine what it could be.

Taking a deep, fortifying breath I imagine Garrick, my big strong soul bond, standing in the Human crowd scaring all the pretentious party goers and I smile knowing he is here for me.

The sharp sound of raised voices filters through my door, making me tense. Corrine and I exchange worried glances as we recognize Bertram's demanding tone.

"She is my betrothed! I have every right—" His volume increases with every word.

"And I am her brother," Cedric's voice cuts through, cold and precise. Relief floods me. He has become a faithful ally, a true brother in the few days I have returned. "You will meet her in the ballroom as is proper. Or shall I inform Father that you lack the basic courtesy expected of a noble house?" My heart sings with joy at Cedric's intervention, I never expected to have a brother fight for me. Cedric is showing he is no longer that little boy but has become a man with strength and integrity.

A long silence follows, Corrine and I standing still in anticipation. Eventually the sound of retreating footsteps—and what I imagine is Bertram's frustrated huff—signal he has left. When Cedric enters moments later, his controlled expression breaks into startled surprise at the sight of my dress.

"Lettie..." He blinks, then a slow grin spreads across his face. "You're wearing a Fae gown," he says, with such glee I can't help but smile.

"Is it too much?" I smooth my hands over the shimmering fabric, a twinge of uncertainty floats to the surface but it doesn't last long.

His grin widens into something almost mischievous. "It's perfect. Father will hate it." Words I never thought would bring me so much joy. He crosses the room and takes my hands in his. "You look absolutely stunning. Like a true princess, not some painted doll." That is the best compliment I have ever heard, well almost. Garrick's compliments are better but this is a true compliment–from my brother, which has never happened before.

"Thank you." I squeeze his hands, grateful for his support. The thread that seems to lead to Garrick pulls at me, anxious to be near him again, but having Cedric beside me helps calm my nerves–this is what family is supposed to be.

"Ready to scandalize the entire court?" He offers his arm with an exaggerated flourish. I release a completely improper laugh, overjoyed to be who I am in front of him.

"As I'll ever be." I take his arm, drawing strength from his steady presence. Whatever happens next, at least I know I'm not alone. I have Cedric, I have Garrick, I even have Milori... and for once in my life, I have hope.

We leave my chambers behind, heading toward the ballroom where my future awaits. The stone floor carries the sound of my heels down its empty and lifeless corridors. The walls are covered in old tapestries describing the time of war and glory, a history filled with hate and injustice.

I have never liked being here, too impersonal and gaudy.

"Cedric, did someone inform Mother I was here?" My earlier concern rising to the surface. The look on Cedric's face says there is more to this than I probably want to know.

"They weren't going to tell her—Father and Rowan—but I pretended I didn't realize the missive wasn't supposed to be sent out and I sent it myself." Defiance and anger shift his features. He's growing into his own, much like I am.

"You're fighting your own battle, aren't you." Not a question, more of a statement and the look in his eyes says all I need to know.

"I should have been fighting it a long time ago. I'm sorry, Alette." His words are laced with pain and regret. I slow us and turn to face him, really looking at the man in front of me and not the memory of the eight year old I helped raise.

He is tall like Father, but has the same shade of hair as me. His facial features are a perfect mix of Mother and Father but there's this look of a young man finding his place in this world. Against all odds he has stopped to think about his own life, and actions, and chose something different.

"When we first spoke in the carriage I didn't know if what you were saying was truthful," He winces at my words, but I continue. "You could have lied to me, used it as a cruel trick to make me feel safe and then destroyed that safety like Rowan would have done... but you didn't. You're a better man than either, and I admire you more for it. To change–really change despite what I am guessing is harsh treatment, especially from Rowan." Just the look in his eyes confirms this is true. "You have become an honourable and amazing man. Thank you for standing with me, for being a support and please do not feel guilty one second more. I forgive you, Cedric, and I love you dearly."

He swallows hard and then pulls me into a tight hug. "I don't know why you were placed in such a wretched family when you're a blessing to so many. I love you, Lettie." He pulls away and we both take a steadying breath. The future may be uncertain but we have each other now, and for that I am grateful.

The rest of our journey to the ball room is quiet and uneventful, a blessing because I need to focus on surviving this evening.

Everywhere I look servants rush about with last-minute preparations—polishing silver sconces, adjusting flower arrangements, lighting fresh candles. The usual suffocating stillness of the castle has given way to nervous energy.

Just before our last turn Cedric fidgets and adjusts his jacket.

"Something odd is happening," Cedric says quietly as we round the corner. "I saw Rowan speaking with someone in the gardens earlier—someone Father doesn't know about."

I glance at him, catching the concern in his expression. "What do you mean?"

"I'm not sure yet. But Rowan's been meeting with people in secret. Whatever he's planning..." Cedric's grip on my arm tightens slightly. "Just be careful, Lettie. I don't trust him." I nod tucking the warning away.

I've never trusted Rowan but to know he is meeting people in secret without Father's knowledge adds another level of concern to it.

Before I can press for more details, we arrive at the grand doors leading to the ballroom. The massive oak panels are carved with scenes of ancient battles—victories of the Human kingdom that Father loves to boast about. Two guards stand at attention, and I can hear the buzz of conversation along with music coming from within.

My heart pounds against my ribs as the herald steps forward. This is it.

"Her Royal Highness, Princess Alette of Windsmere," the herald's voice booms through the ballroom. The doors swing open and all eyes turn to us.

The room falls silent as I enter, the usual whispers giving way to shocked murmurs at my appearance. The whispers make me simultaneously happy and nervous. Every partygoer stares at me with utter shock and horror. Father is beside himself, I can see the redness around his neck at my outfit. I feel Bertram's hungry gaze from where he stands near Father, his eyes raking over me in a way that makes my skin crawl. And Rowan, he just looks disgusted.

I push all of that out of my mind because then, I see him. Across the room, beside a large arched window I see those blue eyes. He stands tall and imposing beside Milori. Everyone nearby gives them a wide berth, likely out of fear. Garrick's eyes darken as he takes in my dress and a buzzing thrill of excitement courses through my body. The look of quiet appreciation strengthens my resolve. I can't help but think about how my dress is the very shade of his wonderful skin. The pulling in my chest becomes tight as if begging me to go to him and walk into his embrace. I fight to keep my expression neutral so as to not give away the joy I feel at seeing him.

The desire in his gaze makes me feel powerful in a way I've never experienced before. For the first time in my life, I'm choosing who I want to be–who I want to be with.

Let them stare. Let them whisper. Tonight, I'm no longer just a bargaining chip in my father's games.

Chapter 16

Alette

My feet move through the steps of yet another dance with Bertram, each turn bringing me closer then farther from where Garrick stands. Though I try to maintain the proper distance between us, Bertram keeps pulling me closer, his grip painfully tight on my waist.

"You look absolutely ravishing in that dress." His breath hits my ear, making me shudder and I don't miss the dip of his eyes. "Though I would have preferred something more... modest. I don't need everyone seeing what is mine so openly. We'll have to work on your wardrobe choices after the wedding."

I try to lean away but his fingers dig deeper into my side. "The colour suits me." My voice comes out steadier than I feel.

"Indeed it does." His eyes rake down my body, lingering too long on the neckline. "I can't wait to peel it off of you on our wedding night." My stomach turns at his words but he continues, his voice dropping lower. "I'll teach you exactly what that pretty mouth of yours is good for. You won't be defying my wishes but begging me—"

"Pardon the interruption," Milori's cultured voice cuts through Bertram's vile whispers. "But I believe court protocol dictates all foreign dignitaries be given a turn with the princess." The look on Milori's face is one of triumph and perfectly disguised fury.

Bertram's face darkens with anger. "We are in the middle of a dance," he states.

"Are we?" Milori's smile is sharp as a blade. Without waiting for a response, he smoothly inserts himself between us, taking my hand and leading me away from Bertram. "My, the air quality seems much improved over here. Wouldn't you agree, Princess?"

A surprised laugh escapes me as we whirl into the next dance. "Thank you," I whisper, grateful for the rescue, a small bit of tension finally releasing from my shoulders.

"Don't thank me yet." His eyes sparkle with mischief. "I'm a terrible dancer. Just ask your hulking green admirer over there. He's been grinding his teeth to dust watching that pompous lord paw at you."

As if summoned by Milori's words, Garrick appears beside us wearing a bronze jacket with matching trousers, using a cream top to pull it all together. My heart leaps at the sight of him, that thread that always seems to lead to him, humming to life.

"Mind if I cut in?" His voice is rough. From anger or longing I don't know.

"Oh, thank the sun." Milori dramatically wipes his brow. "I was about to step on the princess' toes anyway." He gives me a theatrical bow before melting into the crowd.

I notice several nobles huddle together and whisper but I don't care because my big green knight is here right in front of me.

Garrick's large hand engulfs mine as he draws me into the dance. Even through his gloves, I feel the spark of connection. We shouldn't be doing this—it's too dangerous. But as his other hand settles carefully on my waist, erasing the memory of Bertram's grip, I can't bring myself to care.

"You look handsome." I whisper. He shifts a bit awkwardly like he is trying to move the fabric off his skin.

"Milori made me wear it. He said it wouldn't look good if I showed up wearing my normal clothes."

I laugh a bit at his discomfort. "I prefer you in your other clothes. I prefer simple." A flush of heat passes over me. He looks much better wearing his worn, dirty shirts that show off all his muscles and brown leather pants–that I am sure have blacksmithing purposes but I just like the way they look on him.

Something rumbles in his chest which I am taking as a good sign.

"Noted." He smiles at me with a warmth I can't quite handle. "You're wearing my colour," he whispers low, meant only for me.

"I wanted you to see me in it. I wore this at the Night of the Golden Trail but you weren't there... so I wore it tonight," I confess. He looks sad at my admission but he smiles warmly. "Even if we can't..."

I don't finish the sentence. While I have been enjoying my small moment with him, I begin catching several eyes watching us intently. *Right, I can't act too friendly.* His jaw clenches, and even as we spin around the dance floor I can feel the tightness in his body.

"I want to kill him," he whispers and that statement alone scares me while also providing me comfort. "But no matter what, my little ember, I am always here ." The promise wraps around me like a warm blanket.

The music swells around us as we move together, and for just a moment, I let myself imagine a different life. One where I could dance with him openly, where I didn't have to pretend his touch doesn't set my soul on fire. But across the room, I catch Bertram's murderous glare, and reality comes crashing back. This stolen moment can't last forever and that is emphasised by the slowing of the music. The song changes and I know to dance with him for another song would be improper.

"Go, I'm right here." I feel the strain as he asks me to leave but he's right; I need to return to Bertram.

He bows deeply before straightening to his full height again as he walks back to his post at the window, the crowd opening wide to give him room. Returning to Bertram feels like the prick of a thousand needles but I hold myself high when I finally make my way back to him.

"Are you okay, my dear? Disgusting thing... touching you like that. If this were at my estate he would be dragged outside and hung for even thinking about touching you!"

He says all this loud enough for his friends to comment and encourage such awful speech. He takes another large drink of his wine, laughing with his acquaintances. How much has he had to drink? I say nothing, clasping my hands tight together trying to fight back the need to yell at him for saying such awful things about Garrick. This isn't the time or place to make that stand.

The night drones on as more people come up to us and congratulate our upcoming wedding. Bertram talks incessantly about how lucky I am to be marrying him and how the kingdom is lucky to be joining with the Blackthorn house. It will bring great strength to the kingdom.

I want to vomit from all the arrogant things he says.

"Come, my dear. I believe we need some... private time." Bertram's fingers dig into my arm as he pulls me away from some nobles he has been talking to. The men smirk at our departure and my stomach sinks. He pulls me roughly toward one of the side exits.

"I should really stay—the guests—" Panic claws at my throat as I search desperately for an excuse. Even a stray eye from another noble woman might give me enough of an excuse to stay

"The guests can wait." His voice is sharp and his grip tightens painfully. "You seem to have forgotten who's in control here.

Best you learn now, before the wedding." My heart races at his threat.

I frantically look around but everyone just seems to ignore us. I can't see Garrick in the crowd and my body begins to rebel against this force.

I try tugging my arm gently but Bertram responds with an even tighter grip, the pain nearly making me call out.

Bertram practically drags me into the dimly lit corridor. The music from the ballroom fades as the door shuts behind us. All I can hear now is the sound of my rapid breathing and his angry muttering.

"Prancing around in that indecent dress... making me wait... thinking you can do whatever you want..." His words slur together, the wine on his breath making me nauseous. "It's time you learned your place."

Without warning, he shoves me against the wall. My head cracks against the stone, stars exploding behind my eyes. His hand wraps around my throat, not quite squeezing but threatening as he brings his face inches from mine.

"Please—" The word comes out strangled as terror freezes my blood.

"Such a pretty mouth." His other hand grips my jaw roughly. "Always saying 'no' when you should say 'yes'." His words are sloppy.

I try to twist away but he's too strong, his body pressing mine into the wall. He shoves his leg into me to prevent me from moving. I push wildly on his chest to move, but it doesn't help–it just makes him angrier.

When his mouth crashes against mine, I bite down hard. The sharp tang of wine mingles with the metallic taste of blood, flooding my senses and making me want to wretch it all away.

He jerks back with a snarl. "You little—" His hand moves from my jaw back to my throat and it tightens impossibly.

"Help!" I manage to cry out before his grip cuts off my air. "Someone plea—" Dots invade my vision as I lose the ability to speak. Completely terrified, I know this is inevitable; if no one has heard me yet they won't hear me at all.

Suddenly the pressure vanishes and I am gasping for air. My vision slowly returns, the spots fading but what I see before me is more terrifying. Garrick stands over Bertram who has been tossed to the floor and before I can say anything Garrick's large fist comes down on him.

Chapter 17

Garrick

Being surrounded by all these nobles and their stuck up attitudes might actually make me punch the wall. The constant gossip and judgment seems worse here than in Sonas... though to be fair, it is equally as prevalent there. But, usually at a party they're more concerned about having fun than going off to the side and insulting their neighbour.

"Stop grunting, I can only explain to these Humans so many times, it's because you swallowed something the wrong way." Milori smiles at a passing noble despite taking the time to chastise me.

"I wouldn't grunt if you didn't make me wear this uncomfortable outfit and I could have my soul bond next to me." The thought of Alette instantly makes me look for her to make sure I can see her. That's the only thing that has been keeping the rage at bay, being able to know where she is.

"Oh, stop it. Even Emilia would have made you put something nice on. You're such a Orchy fusspot."

Milori mutters on but I've stopped listening. I can't find Alette. Moving through a few nobles, I search the ballroom for my little ember but I can't see her dark green dress in the sea of pastel ones. Where did she go?

My rage comes thundering to the surface and I clench my fists to control it.

"What's the matter?" Milori is beside me, concern etched in his voice.

"I can't find Alette," I growl out. Milori doesn't tease me or comment on how I'm acting like a brute because we both agreed we would keep an eye on her tonight. Something about Bertram made us think he might try something tonight.

My nerves are already frayed just having to attend this event but losing sight of her is lighting them on fire—nothing is going to stop me from finding my soul bond. A cursory scan across the room confirms she's not in here.

I catch Cedric's eye and it looks like he is searching for her too. I start moving in the direction of where I last saw her.

"Garrick, wait—" Milori tries to stop me, probably concerned about keeping up appearances but something feels wrong. The bond pulls tight at my chest, something is very, very wrong.

The crowd parts as I walk towards the far corner where she once stood. Now, in her place is a group of male nobles who are laughing and sipping wine.

"Where is she?" My voice carries the menace that I feel.

The nobles back up, scared by my presence. Good, they should be. I don't need to tell them who I am looking for. I think our dance explained a little too much but I don't care. They all seem to mutter to themselves. I lean in, about to grab one of them, when the smaller one speaks up.

"They went back there."

He points to a door in the back. Even though I want to punch every single one of them, I barge past them to head for the door. When I push open the door, the sight before me ignites a fury so intense my blood feels like molten metal. Bertram has Alette pinned against the wall, his hands forcefully restraining her, violating everything sacred about her. Red bleeds into my vision, primal rage consuming every rational thought.

"Help!"

Her desperate, pained cry shatters something inside me, and I'm moving before my mind can even process what's happening.

Every protective instinct roars to life. All I can see is the threat to my soul bond, and in that moment, I know this man will not survive what he's done. Her strangled plea for help fuels the darkness growing within me, promising swift and brutal retribution.

My hands find Bertram's collar, ripping him away from Alette with a force that sends him sprawling across the floor. The rage consuming me is beyond reason, beyond control. The beast that everyone fears, the brutal and vicious Orc they are so terrified of will not be held back.

Before he can even attempt to recover, I'm on him. My massive frame blocks out what little light filters into the corridor.

"Please—" Bertram tries to scramble backward, his perfectly polished shoes scrabbling against the stone floor. But there's no escape. Not from me. Not after what he tried to do to my soul bond.

My first punch connects with a sickening crunch. Blood sprays from his nose, splattering across his face. He tries to raise his hands to protect himself, a weak attempt, as there is nothing he can do to stop me.

"Stop!" he chokes out, blood and spittle flying from his mouth with each word. "You'll be executed for this!"

I don't care. Each blow is for every moment of fear Alette has endured. For every time she's been treated like a possession. For the bruises that are likely forming on her delicate throat.

Another punch. And another.

His face becomes a mess of blood and broken nobility. He begs but I don't hear it. It merely encourages me to keep going. He thinks he can touch an Orc's soul bond? The darkness inside me demands retribution.

"Please..." Bertram's pleas become weaker, more desperate.

The only thing that seems to cut through the haze is a delicate voice, a scared and delicate voice. My body goes still and I hear it.

"Garrick, please. Stop." Alette. She's terrified and I am acting like a wild animal. Bertram's weak, barely conscious body hangs from my grip. His eyes are already swollen and his nose and lip bleed from the beating.

I drop him to the ground, my body heaving from the exertion.

Alette comes over to me while I'm frozen in place. One move, I fear, will send me into a rage again but then her hazel eyes are in front of me and the bond is desperate to hold onto her... She must be afraid of me.

I look at my blood covered hands, I can't seem to look up at her.

"Hey, everything's alright. I'm right here." She places her hands on my face, forcing me to look at her. My body relaxes at the lack of fear in her eyes, my shoulders drop knowing she is right here.

It's then that I notice a lot of noise and people shouting.

"That's enough." Milori's commanding tone cuts through the corridor just as the thunder of armored footsteps approaches. Guards pour in from both directions, weapons drawn. "Stand down, all of you!"

Milori has positioned himself in front of Alette and I as a crowd from the ball room has come into the corridor. As the guards are surrounding us, I tuck Alette behind my back while that earlier rage fans back to life.

Red flames dance along Milori's hands as he steps between the guards and me, every inch the king's captain. The corridor falls silent as the king arrives, his sons trailing behind him.

"Your Majesty," Milori declares, his voice cutting through the tension, "I must formally report a serious incident involving a royal guest under diplomatic protection."

The king's eyes narrow, taking in Bertram's bloodied form and the scene before him. Before he can speak, Milori continues, "Lord Bertram was caught attempting to assault Princess Alette—his own betrothed—in a most heinous manner. My companion, Garrick, brother to Queen Emilia of the Day Court, intervened to protect the princess when no one else would." His words command in the darkened corridor.

"He attacked a noble!" One of the guards shouts, the disgust for me clear. The king's face begins to turn red with anger.

Milori's gaze sweeps the room, his flames casting an otherworldly glow. "A noble who was in the process of sexually assaulting the princess. Are you prepared to explain to King Timas why you're defending such actions? After he rescued her from the Night Court?" The implied threat hangs heavy in the air. "As representatives of the Day Court, we are honour-bound to protect those who cannot protect themselves." He steps forward, maintaining a position between the guards and me. "The marks on the princess' throat speak for themselves. This is a matter of royal protection and diplomatic protocol. I demand a full investigation into Lord Bertram's actions."

The king sputters, "Silence! I will not have you—"

"With all due respect, Your Majesty," Milori interrupts, his voice deadly calm, "I am here officially representing King Timas, who specifically asked to be informed of the princess' well being. The brother of his queen has witnessed an assault on the royal princess. Unless you wish to explain to King Timas why you are protecting a man who attempted to force himself on your own daughter, I suggest we proceed carefully."

The corridor is thick with tension. The guards exchange nervous glances, fully aware of the potential diplomatic nightmare unfolding.

"Father, please—" Alette steps out from behind me and it takes everything in me not to pull her back. She steps further into the light where you can see the bruises that disgusting whelp left behind.

"But look at her neck!" Cedric interrupts, pointing to where the purple and brown bruise sits at her neck "Surely you can see—"

"What I see," the king cuts in, voice deadly quiet, "is an Orc who has attacked a noble of my court. Take him to the dungeons." He waves dismissively at the guards. "I will deal with my daughter later."

"Your Majesty," Milori steps forward, blue flames still dancing along his hands. "As representative of King Timas, I must insist—"

"You may insist on nothing in my castle." The king's eyes narrow dangerously. "Your... companion has violated our hospitality. Be grateful I don't have him executed where he stands."

The guards move to grab my arms. Every instinct screams to fight, to get back to Alette, but I force myself still. Fighting now will only make things worse. The bond rages as they pull me away, but I keep my eyes locked on Alette. I need her to know I would do it again—a thousand times over—to keep her safe. Tears pour down her cheeks and I nearly throw the guards who have me against the wall to get to her... But I can't, for her I can't.

"I'll handle this," Milori says quietly as they lead me past. His determined face says he is going to fight and that brings me some peace. "Trust me."

And I do.

Rowan watches with barely concealed satisfaction while Cedric has gone to Alette and has her wrapped in his arms protectively. But all I can focus on is her face, growing smaller as they drag me toward the dungeons.

"Come," I hear the king demand roughly. "We will discuss your... behaviour in private."

I look at Milori again and he nods as if to say he will stay with her. The only hope of peace I have is that she may have some protection with Cedric and Milori.

I did not expect this evening to end like this but I would do it again, to protect her.

Chapter 18

Garrick

Not sure how long I've been down here but the tiny cell feels like it's getting smaller with every short pass I make. A small barred window is the only light coming into the cell, the moon hanging high in the sky. Even the diminutive lantern on the wall outside my prison doesn't illuminate much.

I can't stop thinking about her, if she's okay–if she is safe. My hands shake with the need to do something, anything.

Her cry for help will haunt me till the end of my days. How could I have lost sight of her? What kind of soul bond does that? I continue to fail her and I'm suffocating under it.

"By the sun, you look terrible." Milori stands in front of my cell, the single light casting an orange glow on his face. I walk quickly to the door eager to know how Alette is. His teasing tone is gone when he gets a good look at me.

"Is she okay?" I don't hide the fear in my voice. She is somewhere in this castle and I can't get to her to ensure she is safe.

"She's shaken up but she is more concerned about you than anything else. She said ,and I quote, 'Please tell him I'm alright and that I don't regret a single moment. Tell him he saved me in more ways than just tonight, and I won't let him face this alone'." Milori's usual playful demeanor softens as he delivers her message. "She's quite something, your little ember."

"I should grab you and toss you across the room for using her pet name," I growl with no bite.

"Ah, but you can't with those little bracelets on." I look at the chains they have wrapped around my wrists. Not surprising they have strong Orc iron in their prison.

I let out a heavy sigh resting my head on the bars. I'm agitated, tired, and away from my soul bond which is not improving my mood.

"You really made quite the mess up there." I look up at him as he examines his nails with exaggerated care. "Though I must say, you did a spectacular job rearranging Bertram's face. The healers say he'll live—unfortunately. Though eating might be difficult for a while with that broken jaw."

I rumble out a satisfied grunt, then my lips twitch despite myself. The memory of Bertram's perfect noble features crumpling under my fist brings a savage satisfaction.

"Honestly, I'm surprised they couldn't do more for him. Is this what it's like to live somewhere without magic? Not that I think he should be relieved of any discomfort but what a primitive way to live." Milori shivers.

"Not everyone has magic to instantly heal wounds. Some races have to do it the natural way."

"Barbaric," he mutters. "Anyways, that wasn't the plan, you know." Milori's voice loses its playful edge. "You were supposed to avoid getting arrested, remember? Hard to help Alette from down here."

"What was I supposed to do?" I grip the bars firmly, my green skin nearly splintering from the jagged metal. "Just let him do whatever he wanted..." I know Milori would never agree to that but I am not going to apologize for protecting my soul bond.

"No." He leans against the wall across from my cell and I see the exhaustion in his eyes. He has been working tirelessly to help me, I know that. "But we literally talked about you avoiding the dungeons. Though, I can't say it wasn't satisfying to see you destroy that pompous man's face. To be honest, I am not sure I would have been able to show that much restraint." He pushes his hand through his hair in frustration.

"I would have kept going if Alette hadn't been there." The words are true, had she not asked me to stop I would have killed him.

"I've sent word to Timas. He and Emilia should be here within a day." The casual statement raises new fears for me.

"You brought Em into this?" The chains rattle as I shake the bars. "This place isn't safe for her."

"Oh yes, because your little sister—you know, the *queen* of the most powerful Fae court—is some delicate flower—yes, that was an intentional word choice—who can't handle herself." He rolls his eyes dramatically. "Besides, do you really think Emilia was going to let Timas come here without her while her brother is in jail? No, no she would not. And we both know Timas would destroy this place if one single pinky touched his spirit

bond or did you forget what he did in Ezuren? That overpro-
tective idiot barely lets her walk the gardens alone."

He's right. I know he's right but the people I care about—the
people I love—are coming to a place I can't even attempt to
protect them from.

"I just...I just don't think what little sanity I have left can
handle someone else I care about getting hurt because I wasn't
able to stop them." The words feel raw coming out but I can't
help but say it. Milori's look of understanding, lack of judgment
or sympathy, makes me feel a little better.

"I understand. We can always hope that when Timas shows
up he sends a bolt of lightning through the king's chest." That
stupid smirk on his face nearly forces a smile but the recollection
that we're still in a very difficult position right now stifles it.

"Milori—"

"I know, I know, no killing people immediately." He waves
dismissively. "Though you have to admit, it would make this
easier." A familiar glint enters his eye. "But perhaps I can offer
something to improve your mood in the meantime."

Before I can ask what he means, the scrape of stone on stone
echoes through the dungeon. Milori looks in the opposite direction he entered and watches someone walk down the hall. I
hear small clicks echo along the walls. My heart lurches when I
finally see her, my little ember.

Alette rushes forward, her green dress rustling against the
stone floor as she reaches for me through the bars. My hands

find hers instantly, the bond singing at her touch and the constant rage finally starting to settle.

"What are you doing here?" I whisper fiercely, torn between joy at seeing her and terror for her safety. "If they catch you—"

"Shh." She pulls something from the folds of her dress—a key glinting in the dim light. "Thomas—one of the guards—he's helped me before. He gave me this." Her hands tremble slightly as she reaches for the lock.

"Alette, no." My heart pounds against my ribs. If she is thinking about breaking me out... this will be a far greater problem than we already have. "You can't risk—"

"I'm not breaking you out." She looks up at me with those fierce hazel eyes that first captured my soul. "I just... I need to be near you. Please, I need to be close to you with no barriers." The lock clicks open despite her trembling hands. The door squeaks as it opens.

How can I deny her anything when she looks at me like that? The moment she steps into the cell, I pull her into my arms, chains and all. She fits perfectly against me, like she was made to be there. The bond hums with contentment as I bury my face in her hair.

"I'll watch this hallway," Milori says from his post. "Cedric's got the other end. You have some time. Don't do anything I wouldn't do."

He winks at me and I would love to throw something at him but that would require letting go of Alette and I won't do that. I scoop up Alette, drawing a quiet squeak as I cradle her in my arms. The chains drag on the ground as I sit on the prison bed barely larger than a bench. I hold her tightly against me, the darkness that seems to linger at the edge of everything wanes having her so close to me.

She leans her head against my shoulder, her hand playing with the shirt that was ripped open after Bertram tried to grab me during our... encounter.

"Thank you," Alette whispers, not moving from my embrace. I hold her tighter, memorizing every detail of this moment—her warmth, her scent, the way she trembles slightly in my arms. She is here with me and safe.

"My brave Little Ember," I murmur into her hair. "I'm sor—"

"Don't." She sits up to look at me, her voice tight with barely contained emotion. "Don't you dare apologize for saving me, for protecting me."

"I should have been there sooner, should have seen you go so it wouldn't have gotten that far." I lightly trace a bruise around her neck and I regret not killing him.

"You came exactly when you should have. Thank you," she whispers, tears dancing at the edge of her eyes. "If anything I should be sorry. You came here and all you have faced is prejudice... and now a dungeon, perhaps you were—" I lean in and kiss her soft lips, it's slow and intimate. I pull back to take in her features.

"That is never something for you to apologize for. Never."

I pull her against me, holding her tightly as she wraps her arms around my neck. This is where she belongs—safe in my arms, though not in this cursed dungeon. I trace my thumb across her cheek, still amazed she doesn't flinch from my touch.

"You, my perfect Human soul bond, you taught me that fear isn't a reason to run. That being afraid doesn't mean you can't also be brave." The chains rattle softly as I draw her closer. "I have many regrets, Little Ember, but never will I regret being your soul bond and never will I regret falling in love with you." The shock on her face breaks my heart. "Yes, my little ember, I love you and no it's not only the bond... at least it's mostly not just the bond." We both laugh. "But it's you. Your fierce determination, your kind and gentle soul that seems to temper my hard one, your smiles that can't compare to a million suns, it's you."

"I love you too, Garrick. I don't know how but I do. I don't want to live without you and I won't. I will not marry anyone, unless it's you."

My heart burns with affection for this woman. Someone who shouldn't have been bonded to a half Orc like me, someone who deserved better... but she chooses me. "I'll show you every day of my life that you are everything, I promise."

She leans in and kisses me, not the gentle kiss from before but one of eagerness, and I consume her. We get lost in the moment for a long while before I simply hold her in my arms. I don't know how much time passes but she begins to breathe lightly and I know she has fallen asleep. I want nothing more to hold her knowing she feels safe in my arms, to sleep, but this is no place for my little ember. Though I may kill him later, there is only one thing to do.

"Milori," I whisper, loud enough that his Fae hearing should be able to hear me. Sure enough, he walks back to the cell door and looks in. That mischievous smile is back and amazingly I refrain from insulting his ugly face, another miracle today.

"Do I get to take the princess back to her chambers!" He practically jumps up and down with glee. He walks in and I have to control my breathing as he comes closer.

"Protect her with your life." I vehemently say. He drops his crooked smile, the seriousness of my tone sobering him.

"With my life... brother." His words hit me hard. This ridiculous man, who has been annoying since the first day I met him, has become... my brother. He may act like a child and insults me often but somewhere in there he's shown me he is trustworthy, and family. As he gently takes her from my arms I know he will protect her with his life just as I would.

He walks out of the cell with my very soul while Cedric stands to the side to let them out. He closes the door and locks it again, giving me a quick nod as he leaves.

The distant echo of dripping water is all I hear after they leave. I just hope when Timas gets here he can do something because staying away from her forever is impossible now. I will become a beast to get her back.

Chapter 19

Alette

Father's private study feels more suffocating than usual this morning. Heavy curtains block most of the sunlight, as if he wants to keep any form of joy out of the room. The candles give an eerie ambience to the room instead of the inviting one they usually give.

It's a smaller room compared to others in the castle, and set aside specifically for any private dealings Father doesn't want others to know about. It has its own corridor with no rooms on either side to give the most privacy possible.

I stand before Father's massive desk, my hands clasped tightly behind my back to hide how they tremble. The bruises on my neck throb slightly and it hurts to swallow but I know it could be worse. I am grateful to be standing here in one piece despite the events of last night.

The memories of that moment come flooding back. The way he pushed me, grabbed my throat, but I also remember Garrick's power. His large form standing over a bloodied Bertram. The proper part of me demands that I should feel sorry for how badly he was beaten, but I simply don't.

My heart aches knowing Garrick's locked in the dungeons for protecting me. I also can't believe I fell asleep on him last night. I went to comfort him, to show him I would support him—always—and then I fell asleep. Another feeling that stays with me; how he's so warm and so safe. But that issue is now shadowed by this, now I must face Father and whatever he deems is the most appropriate next step.

"Do you have any idea what you've done?" Father's voice cuts through the silence, and I try to refrain from flinching at his tone. He doesn't look up from the papers spread across his desk, as if I'm not even worth his full attention. "The shame you've brought to this family?" Shame?! I brought this shame! Is he kidding?

Rowan lounges in one of the leather chairs by the fire, watching with a smirk on his face. He cocks an eyebrow at me as if to say this is going to be fun to watch. My stomach turns with disgust. Luckily, Cedric stands near the door. His insistence on staying, to be as close as he can and give his silent support while Father continues, builds upon the foundation of him being a faithful sibling.

"I didn't do anything wrong." My voice comes out steadier than I feel. The sweat on my hands produces an uncomfortable evidence of how I truly feel. "Lord Bertram attacked me—"

"Silence!" Father slams his hands on the desk, finally looking up from his papers to glare at me. His very body shakes with anger. "You deliberately provoked him, parading around in th at... that foreign trash. And now an Orc has assaulted a noble of my court."

"He was protecting me!" The words burst out before I can stop them. "Bertram tried to—"

"I said silence!" Father rises, his shadow falling over me. Fear tries to claw at me but I am more determined than ever to stand up for myself. "This is exactly why women cannot be trusted to make their own decisions. Too emotional, too weak to understand what must be done for the good of the kingdom."

I flinch at his words but refuse to back down. The memory of Garrick's gentleness, his love, gives me the strength I never knew I had. "Is that what Mother needed? Someone to make her decisions for her until she finally broke?"

He moved quicker than I expected, the crack of his hand across my face echoes in the quiet room. I hold back the cry of pain, my hand going to my now throbbing cheek. My cheek burns, but I keep my chin held high. I've endured worse. The thought sends another wave of gratitude toward Garrick—he sees my worth when my own family never has.

"You dare?" Father's voice drops dangerously low. "After everything I've done for you?"

"Everything you've done for me?" The words taste bitter on my tongue. A fire burns bright in his eyes. "Like trading me to the highest bidder? Or like how you locked Mother away? Wait, was that best for her or for me? " My heart pounds in my chest. Standing up to my father like this is terrifying but I don't want to be afraid anymore.

"Careful, sister." Rowan's smooth voice carries a threat. "You forget your place."

"My place?" Something snaps inside me. Maybe it's the bond that is making me feel so brave, maybe it's years of bottled up rage, or maybe it's simply knowing what real love feels like. "My place was supposed to be safe in my own home. Instead, you arranged my marriage to a man who tried to force himself on me!" My voice cracks with emotion.

"Enough!" Father's roar makes the candles flicker, and the tremble I have tried to keep at bay comes out in full force. "Lord Bertram was well within his rights. You are his betrothed—"

"That doesn't give him the right to hurt me!" My voice breaks on the last word. Cedric moves closer, but Father's glare stops him.

"The wedding will proceed as planned." Father huffs out. He walks back around his desk and sits back down with a mind made up. "We'll say the Orc attacked, unprovoked and driven mad by some savage bloodlust. The Day Court can't protest too much if we execute one of their pet monsters."

Ice floods my veins. "No." The word comes out barely above a whisper.

"What did you say?" Father's eyes narrow dangerously.

"I said no." My voice grows stronger. "I won't marry him. And if you hurt Garrick, King Timas will—"

"Will what?" Rowan stands, moving like a snake to Father's side. "Start a war over one half-breed Orc? Please. The Day Court won't risk their precious peace for something so worthless. Especially with this Fae group attacking across the continent. They will need to focus their attention there."

"You underestimate them, brother." Cedric's quiet words draw everyone's attention. "Queen Emilia won't stand idly by while her brother is executed. Besides, the attacks are happening on our land, not theirs. They do not have any vested interest in dealing with them. The Fae group is our issue that we aren't dealing with. You are threatening to kill the queen's brother."

"The Queen?" Father scoffs. "That common-born creature who somehow bewitched King Timas? She should be grateful we even acknowledge her claim to nobility. As for the Fae issue... it is their problem, they were the ones to unleash those rebels onto our land. If they hadn't invaded the shrouded forest we wouldn't have these issues."

"Father, the invasion of the shrouded forest rescued Alette." Cedric steps forward, his voice careful but firm. "Perhaps we should consider working with—"

"I'm beginning to wonder if that was a good outcome." Father cuts him off and glares in my direction. "Are you suggesting we work with them? We are Human, we do not need to bend to the likes of those creatures. This is my kingdom and I will not be told how to run it. No, the Orc dies at dawn tomorrow. And you," he points at me, "will marry Lord Bertram as planned. Then perhaps you'll learn proper obedience." My ears thunder with my anger.

"If you kill him," my voice shakes with fury and fear, "I'll tell everyone what really happened. Every noble house will know you forced your daughter to marry a man who attacked her–that you executed the person who saved her."

"You wouldn't dare." With those words I see the first flicker of uncertainty in my father's eyes.

"Wouldn't I?" I lift my chin. "I have nothing left to lose."

He slings his last attempt at making me back down, "They won't believe you anyways."

"Perhaps you have nothing tangible left to lose, but you could certainly lose your life. Accidents happen all the time." Rowan's malicious threat hangs heavy in the air.

Cedric moves closer to me, about to say something, when the doors to the study burst open. A guard stumbles in, face pale with panic. "Your Majesty! King Timas—he's here. With his queen, and a full diplomatic envoy."

Father's face drains of color. For the first time in my life, I see real fear in his eyes.

"How..." he starts, but I already know; Milori sent word last night. Father thought they wouldn't get here quickly but his arrogance forgets—the Fae king can fly.

"Well, Father," I say, unable to keep the satisfaction from my voice. "It seems we're about to find out exactly what the Day Court will do for someone they consider family."

Hope blooms in my chest. They're here. Help has come. And maybe, just maybe, I'll finally be free of this cage. But if I'm not, they will do everything to get Garrick out and that will give me enough joy to endure more.

***

The throne room feels electric with tension. Father sits rigidly on his throne, his white-knuckled grip on the armrests betraying his unease. I stand at the bottom left, with Cedric by my side, while Rowan takes his place as Father's right hand.

The room is large enough to hold the entire court, the space is nicely splashed with the light of large, elegant candelabras. The stone walls have seen centuries of kings and courts but it's not everyday that the Fae King of the Day Court shows up for a visit. Actually, I am not entirely sure this has ever happened before.

The doors swing open with enough force to rattle the hinges. King Timas strides in, power rolling off him in waves that make the very air crackle. His black hair seems to absorb the light, and his eyes burn with fury. Beside him, Emilia's usual warmth has been replaced by an icy rage that reminds me she was raised by Orcs.

"Your Majesty." Timas' voice carries the weight of a storm. "I received disturbing news about an incident at your engagement ball. It seems my queen's brother intervened to protect Princess Alette from assault by her betrothed and somehow ended up in your dungeons." He vibrates with power and danger. My preconceived security that he won't do anything to me is the only measure keeping me from being terrified.

Many of the nobles here today cower at his presence but he has his eye on my father.

Father rises slowly, clearly trying to maintain control. He begins to weave his lie, "A misunderstanding. The Orc attacked Lord Bertram without provocation—"

"The bruises on your daughter's throat suggest otherwise." Milori steps forward, the look on his face could kill someone and his tone makes it hard to miss the ominous truth he speaks. "As captain of the Fae guard I will not defy my duties and oaths. I stand before you a witness to Lord Bertram forcing himself onto Princess Alette. Garrick reached her before I did or else I would have been the one to forcibly remove him from the princess and not my queen's brother."

"These are internal matters." Father's face reddens. "You have no authority—"

"By your own kingdom's laws," Milori interrupts smoothly, "any betrothal contract is void if one party commits violence against the other. Or perhaps you'd prefer we discuss how your guards failed to protect a royal princess in your own castle? How Princess Alette was dragged past not one but two guards to get to the corridors."

"Words can be twisted to better reflect those laws." Father's voice hardens. "This is my kingdom, and on my authority—"

"A kingdom that seems to be on the brink of civil unrest." The Fae king's power crackles through the air. "We've traced recent attacks along your borders to rebel Fae groups. Groups that are not affiliated with my court... Which begs the question, why have you not sought out our help in this matter, or dealt with it on your own to show the strength of your kingdom?"

His tone stays measured but power ripples beneath each word, making the very air vibrate with barely contained energy. The implied criticism is clear–the Human king is either too weak or too proud to protect his own people.

"These are internal matters," the king repeats himself, his voice sharpened by anger. "Your court's rejects wreak havoc on my lands, and you dare question my handling of it? The only reason these rebels plague us at all is because you drove them from the shrouded forest. This is your mess, spilling onto my kingdom."

The tension crackles between them–two kings, two very different kinds of power. One commanding ancient magic that makes the very stones beneath our feet hum, the other clinging to Human authority that seems to grow more fragile by the day.

"Because, Father," Cedric steps forward, his voice carrying clear across the chamber, "House Silverbrook's ravens arrived this morning. The rebels burned three of their granaries. Houses Moonvale and Thornheart are mobilizing their forces, claiming you've failed to protect the people." Rowan's head snaps toward Cedric, but he continues, "Lord Camden of House Dawnridge arrived an hour ago with concerning reports about unrest in the southern provinces. Houses Windcrest and Stormhaven have already pledged to stand with whoever protects the people's interests." He pauses meaningfully. "And now the heir to House Blackthorn has been exposed attempting to assault a princess while your guards did nothing."

I stare at my younger brother in awe. He's been gathering allies, I realize. Preparing for this moment.

"Duke Blackthorn's support—" Father starts but King Timas cuts him off

"Seeing as you are not only incapable of protecting your people, you are unable to protect the princess. I feel honour-bound to provide such security for her. So, while we work through this issue of assault, she will remain with us." The Fae king's voice brooks no argument. "Her safety clearly cannot be guaranteed here."

"How dare you claim—" Father rises, but Timas' power flares, lightning crackles off him, he is a cloud full of energy ready to destroy at any moment. The nobles step further away and even Rowan takes a step back.

"I dare much more than that." Timas steps forward, his voice deadly quiet. "You arranged her marriage to a man who attempted to assault her. You imprisoned the brother of my queen, who—might I remind you—was here under diplomatic protection. A member of the Day Court's royal family, arrested without trial or evidence while protecting a princess from assault." His power crackles dangerously. "Tell me, what exactly is stopping me from declaring this a hostile action against the Day Court?"

"The wedding contracts—" Rowan tries to interject.

"Are void." Milori speaks for the first time, his cultured voice carrying effortlessly. "Or shall we discuss further how spectacularly your house has failed to protect those under its care?"

"Alette stays with me." Emilia's voice rings with authority. "Or I'll personally visit every noble house in your kingdom to tell them exactly who their king is. I'm sure they'd be fascinated to hear how you treat your daughter." Her eyes flash dangerously. "After all, I have some experience with how the nobility treats those they consider beneath them, but I know of many who have a significant amount of power in this kingdom who would be very interested to know this."

Father's face has gone from purple to white, and I see the defeat in his eyes. He knows he's cornered. Not just by the Day Court's power, but by his own kingdom's growing unrest.

"The choice," Timas says softly, "is yours. But choose carefully. The consequences will be... significant."

I hold my breath, watching Father's perfect world crumble around him. For the first time in my life, I see him for what he truly is—a small man desperately clinging to power he doesn't deserve.

"She may go." The words seem to physically pain him. "Temporarily. Until this... situation... is resolved."

"Now, on the topic of my brother." Emilia's voice cracks like a whip. "Release him, now."

Father internally fights with whether he wants to truly fight this but Timas and Emilia have the upper hand. With a quick glance to one of the guards he waves weakly. "Bring the Orc."

"Garrick," Emilia corrects coldly. "His name is Garrick."

Father doesn't reply and miraculously he doesn't pull a face at Emilia, I am sure Timas would have an instant reaction for that.

Emilia fixes her eyes on me, a warm smile on her face and she waves me over. I quickly look at my father , not allowing his death stare to bother me. I walk quickly over to her and she wraps me up in her arms.

"I'm so sorry, Alette. I should have stopped you from coming back," she whispers in my ear.

I smile at her concern. "You gave me the choice. You could have stopped me but you didn't, thank you," I respond with a whisper.

She pulls back to look at me, the genuine care for me evident in her eyes. "I'm not gonna do that again." I laugh at how serious she is and she smiles in turn.

"Thank you for coming to help." I don't know how to make her understand what it means to me that they came to help.

"We protect our own," she whispers fiercely. "And you, dear sister, are family now." My heart wants to mend back together at her earnest confession. Family... Maybe I can experience what it would be like to have a real family who always loves and cares for me.

The wait for Garrick feels endless. The throne room is quiet except for the whispers from some of the attendants. When the guards finally bring him up from the dungeons, my heart lurches at the sight of him in chains.

I know I saw him last night but it was dark. Now, within the sunlight, I see the dirt that covers him and the rip in his clothes. His hair has fallen out of his normal tie, but he doesn't look defeated; he looks murderous and that makes me more happy than it should.

His blue eyes find mine immediately, that thread tugs tight—a hum in my chest telling me my soul bond is here. He is here, and he is alive.

"Remove those chains." Emilia's voice could cut glass. "Now."

"I may have allowed him to come up from the dungeons but you will not order such things from me. He still assaulted a noble and will have to answer for that crime." Father's last effort at remaining in control is slipping which is evident by how he shrinks in on himself the longer this conversation continues.

"Your Majesty," Timas addresses Leofric, though his tone suggests the title is merely a formality. "Given the complex diplomatic nature of this situation, I propose that while my assembly and I wait for this issue to be resolved, Garrick will be put under house arrest with us as guardians. I do not believe you want to explain to your court why you're imprisoning the Day Court's diplomatic envoy, the Fae queen's brother, during a time of civil unrest."

Milori steps forward, ever the perfect courtier despite the steel in his voice. "Surely the crown has suitable accommodations for visiting dignitaries? Something befitting the king's... generous hospitality?"

I don't miss the way Father's shoulders tense at Milori's words. The word "generous" cuts like a blade–everyone in this room has seen how he treats his own daughter. The implications are clear; either treat us as honored guests and maintain his carefully crafted image of benevolent ruler, or have his true nature exposed to every noble house in the kingdom.

"The East Wing," Rowan suggests smoothly, though his eyes burn with hate. "It's... secure."

"Perfect." Timas' smile doesn't reach his eyes. "We'll require the entire wing, of course. For privacy."

"The entire—" Father starts to protest but Timas' power crackles again, making the very walls shake.

"The entire wing," Timas repeats softly. "With appropriate guards—both yours and mine. To ensure everyone's safety."

Father sinks back in his throne, defeat written in every line of his body. "Very well."

"The chains," Emilia presses. Father hates talking to women in general but to have to answer to one like Emilia, a very large part of me is pleased to watch this.

Father looks at the guard to the left of Garrick and he waves his hand indicating to undo them. The chains fall to the floor and Garrick stretches, which scares the men beside him. The smirk on his face shows he knows exactly what he does to them, but he isn't looking at them, his blue eyes meet mine.

My heart thuds loudly in my chest. I would give anything to run into his arms but I know I need to keep up appearances, at least for now.

"Of course, we'll need time to prepare—" Rowan begins, but Milori cuts him off with a razor-sharp smile.

"Oh, don't trouble yourself. My men are already moving our things." He bows with exaggerated courtesy. "We took the liberty of assuming your legendary hospitality would prevail."

Father's face mottles with rage, but there's nothing he can do. Not with his kingdom teetering on the edge of rebellion and the Day Court's most powerful members standing in his throne room.

"If everything's settled," Timas begins while offering his arm to Emilia, "we'll retire to our chambers. Garrick, Milori, Princess—come."

I move to follow, but Father's voice stops me.

"Remember, daughter," he calls after me, "you still belong to this crown."

I turn back slowly, meeting his gaze. For the first time in my life, I'm not afraid of him.

"No, Father. I belong to myself."

The words feel like freedom on my tongue. With my head high, I walk away from my father's throne, toward the family that chose me.

Chapter 20

Garrick

The moment we enter the East Wing, my control finally snaps. The bond screams for contact after hours of separation, after seeing her stand so brave before that tyrant she calls a father.

Alette has been glancing at me as much as I have been looking at her, but she refrained from coming to me which is likely wise. My soul feels the pain that she is so close yet so far away.

She turns to walk over to me the moment the doors close and I scoop her up into my arms, pulling her tight against my chest. I tuck my head into her neck, breathing in her sweet scent. Her small hands grip my torn shirt as she buries her face into me as well.

"Little Ember," I breathe into her hair. The darkness that's been clawing at my insides since she left last night quiets. She's here. She's safe.

But when she pulls back to look at me, the afternoon light catches her face and fury explodes through my veins. An angry red mark mars her cheek, obviously fresh. Someone struck her.

A growl builds in my chest, the sound inhuman. The darkness surges back, demanding blood. I gently set Alette down, but keep her close. My hands shake with rage as I carefully trace the mark on her face.

"Who?" The word comes out more snarl than speech.

"Garrick." Alette's voice is soft as she places her hand over mine. "I'm alright. This is a minor inconvenience." She tries to placate me but I need to know who.

"Alette, who did this?" She must see I am not going to give up and so she relents.

"Father," she whispers and the boiling in my veins reaches an all consuming level. I want to kill him, completely and utterly destroy him.

She places her soft hands on my face, her hazel eyes beautiful in the sunlight and I see peace there.

"I can't imagine how you're doing right now–especially with what you told me about how not completing the bond can affect your mental state–but please, my darling, please stay here with me." Her words soothe me and I release the tension in my shoulders.

"*He got a pet name quicker than I did.*" Timas mutters and I don't try to hide the smirk on my face.

"Really, Timas. That's your comment on all of this, not that it is the most romantic sight you have ever seen!" Emilia hits Timas in the shoulder as she pretends to chastise him.

"I have done many romantic things, my flower." Timas pulls her closer into her arms.

Ignoring them I look back at my little ember. "I'm sorry." I gently rub her cheek. "We will figure all of this out, I promise."

"I know." She smiles and places a soft kiss on my cheek.

"Your rooms have been prepared," Milori gestures down the hall, finally dropping his casual pose. "Though I took the liberty of having the servants bring up some proper clothes for you, Garrick. Can't have you terrifying the staff in those rags."

"I don't care about clothes." My voice still carries a growl. "I care about keeping her safe." I see understanding in Milori's eyes.

"And that's exactly why we're here," Emilia says firmly. She turns to Alette with a warm smile. "Come, let's get you settled. I imagine you'd like to change as well, not that this dress isn't... lovely and uncomfortable." Alette laughs and tries to step away. After finally being able to see her and hold her, I struggle to let her go.

"I'll be right back," she says gently and I release my hold, though it takes all of me to do so.

"I know where every exit is in this wing," Milori offers, clearly seeing my struggle. "No one gets in or out without us knowing. She'll be safe with Emilia." His words bring me a small amount of comfort but I won't feel truly calm until I know for certain no one is going to take her from me.

The wing is immaculately presented, I'm sure the fear of having the king of Day Court here has encouraged the servants to do their best at preparing it.

I grab my usual shirt and leather pants. Milori had made sure my clothes from before were brought over, and I could not care one bit that they're not suited for the nobles here; if I didn't care in the Day Court, why would I care here. Besides, it's easier to move in my cotton shirt versus those stiff jackets and I don't want anything to hinder me if I need to defend Alette.

The large area where the wing converges sits full of elegant furniture and decorations. Three large, arched doors open up to the balcony on this side. I pace the room until Alette finally emerges from her room wearing one of the Fae gowns she brought from Sonas. The flowing silver fabric suits her far better than the stiff Human styles her father prefers. More importantly, she looks like herself again. Though she still wears the signs of abuse she has endured, her smile is genuine and there is a light in her eyes that eases something in my chest.

Noise from the door leading to the wing draws everyone's attention. I quickly walk over to Alette and draw her close. She may be safe for now, but I still can't trust she will be safe permanently. One of the noble guards from Timas' court walks in, closely followed by Cedric. He looks around carefully before speaking.

"The nobles are restless." Cedric moves closer, keeping his voice low. "House Silverbrook's ravens have been arriving all morning. Three more granaries burned. The southern provinces blame Father for failing to protect them."

"The Fae rebels?" Timas asks sharply.

Cedric nods. "But that's not all. Duke Blackthorn's support is fracturing, though he still holds Duke Hemmet's support. His own vassals are questioning his judgment after what Bertram did. And now..." He glances at Alette. "Now word of how the king treats his own daughter is spreading."

"How?" Alette asks, tensing in my arms.

"The servants talk. The guards talk. House Moonvale and Thornheart are already calling for changes. If enough noble houses unite, they could force Father to meet some of their demands."

"Including releasing me from the betrothal?" Alette's voice carries a hint of hope.

"Possibly. But Rowan..." Cedric's face darkens. "He's already working to ensure Father's support or rather his own. If Father loses power and is essentially forced to abdicate, Rowan is next in line and I am not sure he would be an improvement from what we have now."

Milori, who's been unusually quiet, suddenly straightens. "Perhaps he is not as much a contender as we all think." He has that shrewd look in his eyes which typically means he has something in the works. "There's something I need to confirm first, but Rowan may not be an issue soon." He glances at Timas, who nods slightly.

"What are you thinking?" I ask, not liking the gleam in his eye.

"Better you don't know yet; plausible deniability and all that." He flashes that insufferable grin. "Try not to start any wars while

I'm gone, or end up in chains again. Though if you do, make sure someone describes it to me in great detail later."

He walks out of the suite with a purpose that I know will either help us or cause us more issues. Either way I trust him, and I know he wouldn't do anything to jeopardize the king or our little makeshift family.

"Will he be alright?" Alette asks softly.

"Milori?" I snort. "That annoying Fae could talk his way out of death itself. He'll be fine."

Before we can delve further into plans with Cedric and Timas, another knock interrupts us. This time it's one of the Human guards, looking distinctly uncomfortable as he hands a sealed message to Timas. His glance becomes a stare at me, the now released Orc who beat the lights out of one of the nobles. After he hands the envelope to one of the noble guards he practically runs out of the suite. Timas silently breaks the royal seal, his expression darkening as he reads.

"It seems we're all summoned to court." His eyes meet mine. "Duke Blackthorn demands justice for his son. The king has agreed to hear the case formally—this afternoon."

"So soon?" Alette starts, but Timas holds up a hand.

"He's trying to handle this before more noble houses arrive." Power crackles in the air around him, Timas is not happy. "The more he can control the narrative, the higher the chance he can retain control... but I don't think even that will be enough."

My fists clench at my sides. Of course they want to rush this, but this might be exactly what we need. When they rush they might mess up and we can only hope that is the case.

"Well," Cedric says exasperated, "it seems the noble houses that are already here will have quite a show to witness." The knowing look in his eyes tells me he's already thinking of how to use this to our advantage.

I pull Alette closer, the bond humming protectively. Let them try their courtly games. They have no idea what they're really dealing with.

I just hope Milori finds whatever he's looking for before then. I have a feeling we're going to need every advantage we can get.

Chapter 21

Garrick

There is still a couple of hours until this trial is supposed to happen and I can't keep my mind from racing. This entire situation is one big mess after another. If I hadn't fought the bond we wouldn't be here and Alette wouldn't have been assaulted. She sits on a chair flipping through a book but I don't think she sees the words on the page. She needs something that will relax her.

With my mind made up, I head down the hall.

"And where do you think you're going?" Milori comes out from some random door like he wasn't just standing there like a creep.

"When did you get back?" I grunt.

"I asked my question first. Besides, I think it's more important that we know where the big scary Orc is going—especially right now—when everyone wants to have your head." He crosses his arms and stares at me, not backing down.

"The kitchens. She needs..." I trail off, struggling to explain this need to do something, anything, to bring her comfort.

"Ah." His smile softens into something genuine. "Third door on the left. The servants won't give you any trouble—they're more afraid of us than the king right now."

I grunt in acknowledgment, oddly grateful for his help.

The kitchen staff does indeed scatter when I enter, but one older woman stands her ground, hands on her hips as she eyes me. "I need to make tea," I say gruffly. Her eyebrows shoot up but something in my expression must convince her to help me because she points me towards their stores without argument.

It takes some searching, but I finally find what I'm looking for—the ingredients for that highland frost berry blend Alette loves so much. The teapot is small and finicky, but I manage to get everything in it, while the old woman mutters about how I am doing it. She must have something loose in her head, to mutter under her breath behind the scary Orc's back... I kind of like her.

When I return, carefully carrying the steaming pot and cup on a tray, Alette's eyes light up in recognition.

"Is that..." She trails off as I set the teapot down on the table beside her chair. The small handle on the teapot is useless so I grab the body of it and pour it into the cup.

"Garrick, your hand." She chuckles and tries to take the teapot from me. I rumble my disagreement but I'm smiling at her attempts.

"The forge is hotter than this tiny teapot. I think my hands can handle the heat, but they need bigger teapots for their guests; they're tiny." She laughs again, sending a warmth through my chest. I put that smile on her face and that makes me feel good.

"Silly man. You expect Windsmere to have anything in Orc size." Her cheeks pinken from giggling. She lifts the cup up and smells the highland frost berry blend. "You found my favourite tea!"

"I thought... well, you always seem calmer with tea." I stumble over my words. Slightly unsure if this will really help.

She cradles the cup close, inhaling deeply, and something in my chest eases at the small smile that crosses her face. "You remembered exactly how I like it."

"Of course I did, Little Ember." I settle beside her on the larger chair, drinking in her presence. "I remember everything about you."

Her free hand finds mine, fingers intertwining. The bond hums contentedly at the contact. The fact I fought this was daft, I am so grateful she is willing to try this–to take a chance.

"Thank you," she whispers. "Not just for the tea, but for... everything."

I squeeze her hand gently. "Whatever happens in that throne room, you're not alone anymore. Never again. Even if the worst should pass, Emilia and Timas will take care of you."

She glares at me for a solid minute. "Don't you dare suggest you're getting out of this after we just discussed I get to choose. I may be delusional but nothing is going to happen to you, even if that means we have to escape." She humphs out a breath which makes her look so cute.

"Ok, Little Ember. We will fight." My utterance grows into laughter and I brush a stray hair back behind her ear.

While content with that she leans against me. She sips her tea, and for just a moment, everything else falls away. Let them have their trials and political games. My soul bond is safe beside me, and that's all that matters. If we have to fight, we will.

"As touching as this is," Milori interrupts as he comes out of nowhere again, "they'll be calling us soon."

"We need to put a bell on you. Sneaking up on people is going to get you killed... particularly by me," I grumble out and pull Alette just a bit closer. She laughs at me but sits up despite my urging otherwise.

"Oh, it's hilarious you think you stand a chance. Your delicate little figure can't handle all of this." He motions to his body, as if showing that would intimidate me.

"We could test this theory in the—" A loud knock echoes in the suite and the laughter falls away while we look at the door.

"I guess it's time to play a different game," Milori says as he stalks towards the door.

A different game. Yes, that's all this is; a game.

***

The throne room feels different from this morning—more crowded, more dangerous. Noble houses have gathered like vultures, their rich clothing and jewels don't hide what they truly are, selfish and power hungry.

We follow close behind Timas and Emilia, keeping Alette tight to my side is the only way I am not going to do something like kill some other noble. This entire game is one I don't want to play. But, if being with Alette means I must play it–and play it well so I am free to leave this kingdom with her–so be it.

As impossible as it looks, I know we will figure it out.

The room quiets down as we enter, all eyes turning to watch us come in. One of the nobles stands in front, practically glaring at Emilia. It must be Duke Hemmet. Emilia doesn't pay any attention to him, her focus entirely on the duke pacing up-front–but I am not above such things. While Duke Hemmet looks at me I wave my fingers in an overexaggerated way to say 'hi.' He practically boils with rage, his fists clenching at his side, which only encourages my smirk.

Admittedly, I would also be upset to see one of my daughter's maids as queen of the Day Court now. Especially after that servant had made such a fool out of my daughter, but... I also wouldn't let someone like Lady Dahlia out of the house with how poorly she acts.

We reach the front of the throne room where Duke Black-thorn stands waiting on us, his body radiating with absolute rage. Alette and I take the right hand side of Timas and Emilia as we wait for this farce to be over.

"This beast nearly destroyed my son!" He gestures wildly as he paces before the throne. "Bertram's jaw shattered, his face unrecognizable! The physicians say he may never speak properly again!"

I barely hold in a snort at hearing he may not be able to speak. I think it makes him better, now no poor soul has to hear the arrogant man speak.

The assembled nobles murmur in horror at the new information. Blackthorn plays to the nobles' horror well as he tries to garner their support. "My boy, my heir—attacked by this savage creature in the king's castle! And for what? For protecting his betrothed's honour?"

I bare my teeth at the lie, the darkness surges within me. But this is unlike the one of fighting the bond; this comes from you having insulted the woman I care about. Alette's hand tightens in mine, keeping me grounded even as rage threatens to consume me.

"If this is how the Day Court treats nobility," Blackthorn continues, turning to address the gathered houses directly, "what hope do any of us have? Will we let them send their pet monsters to maim our sons without consequence?"

Rowan isn't far from where Alette and I stand, promptly near the throne. He stares at us, every bit a predator in this game. He is enjoying this show too much but something about how he stands makes me wonder about his true intentions.

"The savage didn't just attack my son—he humiliated him! Beat him until he was unconscious, like some common street thug!" Blackthorn's performance draws more gasps from the crowd. "And now they dare claim that my son didn't have the right to touch his betrothed on the night of their betrothal ball?!" Some of the murmurs are not as encouraging as they were before. Perhaps some are realizing that they don't know exactly what happened.

I want to yell at this fool for suggesting Alette just accept his advances but I know that won't help. Thankfully, Alette stands beside me, her presence calm and steady.

The doors to the throne room open from the side, the footsteps of the king echo against the stone walls. Everyone in the room bows but our small group. The flame in the king's eyes is an inferno of rage, but he manages to keep that under control as he takes his seat on the throne.

Rowan watches everything from his post, a couple of steps down from the king. Cedric stands on the other side with a rigidity that speaks of his unease at the situation.

With everyone getting themselves arranged I step a little closer to Alette, ensuring she is safe–if only for my own peace of mind. Several people at this point have noticed her holding my hand and the look from the king tells me how they feel about that but I won't let go. Not any more.

The king's stoic face surveys the room until a small tick in his eye arrives, the only indication he's surprised by how many noble houses were able to arrive in such a short time. "Duke Blackthorn, you have called for justice. Now, let us hear your petition." His hands land on the carved arms of the throne chair, his large rings cast a glint in the light. He's trying to maintain some sense of an elevated and calm demeanor. I wonder how long that will last.

Blackthorn steps forward, every inch the grieving father. I want to snarl at his overly dramatic display but I refrain... barely.

"Your Majesty, my son—my only heir—lies broken and bloodied because this... this creature," he jabs a finger at me, "attacked him without provocation. I demand the beast's execution, as our laws require for such savage assault on nobility."

Several nobles nod in agreement, but I notice others shift uncomfortably, their eyes drawn to the bruises on Alette's throat. At least not all the Humans here are dumb. An older man—Duke Moonvale, I think Cedric called him—steps forward slightly.

"If I may, Your Majesty," his weathered voice carries clear authority, "shouldn't we hear from the princess herself? These are... disturbing accusations." He glances quickly at Alette, his eyes being drawn to the now purple and brown bruise. I'm proud of my little ember for not covering it up and standing bravely in front of this court.

The king's face darkens, he doesn't want her to speak but before he can get a word out, Alette moves forward, dropping my hand to stand in front of the nobility and her father. My body wants to follow her but her confidence and strength tell me I am not needed, so I will stand behind her for support instead.

"Lord Bertram dragged me from the ballroom against my will the night of our betrothal ball." Her words silence the whispers instantly. "When I refused his advances, he..." her voice catches slightly, but she lifts her chin in defiance of her own emotions. "He pinned me to the wall. Tried to force himself on me. These bruises?" She gestures to her throat. "These came from his hands, not Garrick's. All Garrick has done was prevent Bertram from taking advantage of me. For protecting me when no one else would."

Gasps ripple through the crowd. I know the culture within the Human kingdom is divided when it comes to these sorts of topics but I am happy to see the disgust on so many of their faces. Duke Moonvale's expression hardens as he looks at Blackthorn.

"She lies!" Blackthorn sputters, but another voice joins in—Duke Thornheart. His silver hair gleaming in the afternoon light.

"Does she?" The older man's voice drips with disdain. "I've heard... similar rumors about your son's behavior toward young women before, Blackthorn. Things swept quietly away with coins and threats. It's why he's not invited to many gatherings across the kingdom."

"This is outrageous!" Blackthorn turns to the king. "You can't possibly allow these baseless accusations—"

"I witnessed it myself." Milori steps forward, every inch the king's captain despite his casual stance. "As did several others. The princess' cries for help drew quite an audience—though apparently it wasn't panicked enough for the castle guards to act and protect their own." His words cut like a knife and the audience whispers harshly.

More nobles shift uncomfortably from the statement. The political implications hang heavy in the air—if the king can't protect his own daughter in his own castle, what hope do their children have, their people? Add in the Fae rebels causing issues on their lands and the king is looking less capable of his position.

But Rowan moves to salvage the situation, he takes a step into the centre slightly closer to Alette which makes me uneasy. His smooth voice cuts through the tension. "Surely we can find a... diplomatic solution. One that preserves everyone's honour?"

The rage building inside me finally breaks free and I walk deliberately up beside Alette. No longer will she face these vultures alone. "There is no diplomatic solution that ends with her marrying him." My voice carries through the throne room, making several nobles step back. "She is my soul bond." My chest is heaving with rage and I am sure the sight of me is scaring the poor Humans, but I don't care.

Emilia mutters something that sounds suspiciously like 'Well, there goes subtlety.' but I don't care anymore. I'm done with their games.

The king's face distorts with fury. "You dare claim some sort of ownership over my daughter?"

"Not ownership." Alette's clear voice rings out as she moves to step into me, a move showing she stands with me of her own accord. "A connection that can't be broken by contracts or crowns. One that would drive him mad if you force us apart." She turns to address the court directly. "Do you really want an unstable Orc warrior in your kingdom? Because that's what you'll get if you separate us."

That gets their attention. Not appeals to higher powers or true love, but the practical threat of an enraged Orc. These nobles understand power and consequences.

"That can be easily solved by killing him now." Rowan spits out in disgust. But some of the nobles don't pay attention to him.

"Is this true?" Duke Moonvale asks Timas, clearly seeking his authority on a significant thing such as this.

"Yes." Timas stands taller, his presence commanding respect. "Orcs denied their soul bonds eventually lose all control. From my understanding—because the bond works differently for Orcs—they will lose their humanity and become what all of you fear." The calm delivery of the words unsettles the crowd.

I look at Milori as he sarcastically comments on the situation, "Personally, I wouldn't want an angry Orc running around but that's just me. Very messy business. Though, I'm sure the duke's son would be happy to have such a guest in his lands after the marriage." None within the court mistake his words for playfulness or kindness, he is ready to fight– his body on edge like everyone else's.

Before anyone can respond, the throne room doors burst open. A guard rushes in, face flushed with urgency. "Your Majesty! There's been another attack—Fae rebels have burned the village of Millbrook!"

"Not far from the castle, three more granaries destroyed," another guard adds between breaths. "The villagers... they had no chance to defend themselves."

With that, the room erupts in shouts.

Chapter 22

Alette

My heart jumps into my throat as the shouting continues. The nobles are irate about the recent attack. Garrick wraps his arm around me, grounding me amidst the mayhem.

No longer is this a trial for Garrick and his actions but now a challenge in confidence from every noble house here, questioning Father and what he is going to do about it.

"Your Majesty, my lands border Millbrook!" Duke Wilmsburg states loudly over the voices. Father's face cracks under the shouts, his previous calm and authoritative exterior now one of disbelief and determination to get everything under control.

"How many more must die while we debate petty politics?" Another noble says. Some have taken to yelling at their neighbour about whose lands are more important than another and why.

"The crown does nothing while our people starve!" Angry shouts echo in the room. Father's face, reddened to match, hardens into a mask of steel.

I press closer to Garrick as the noise builds to a deafening roar. His solid presence steadies me even as nobles push and shove around us. Father rises from his throne, face enraged as he tries to regain control of his court.

"SILENCE!" His voice booms across the room but for once, the nobles ignore him. Their fear of the rebels outweighs their fear of the crown.

Father waves his hands instructing the guards to quiet the people. One of the guards has forcibly restrained one of the nobles, the shock of it rippling through the audience. Once the guards surround many of the nobles, they quiet and look at Father.

"These attacks are the work of the Fae, we will ask the Fae king why these are occurring and demand the answers." Father directs his ire at Timas, my body starting to shake. Timas is a powerful man and Father's arrogance is going to get him killed.

The Fae king's features harden and the air begins to crackle around us. Milori steps around Timas, however, and all eyes land on him.

"Actually," Milori's cultured voice cuts through the chaos like a blade, "I believe I can shed some light on these attacks." He steps forward, each stride purposeful and full of intent. The crowd falls quiet, drawn by his commanding presence.

"What could a Fae noble possibly know about this?" Rowan sneers, but something flickers in his eyes.

"First of all, I am no mere noble. I am the king's captain and I make it my business to know anything and everything that would threaten the king. Now as for these particular Fae, they have some motives I think this court might be interested to know. To be clear, these Fae have no association with the Day Court but are rather Night Court rebels seeking what they consider to be justice." Milori looks at Timas and some sort of understanding passes between them. Suddenly he produces a leather folio from his jacket.

"What are you talking about?" My father demands. His patience is gone—if he had any to begin with—but with a room full of agitated nobles demanding answers to the problem at hand, he listens.

"I started my investigation the moment we landed on the continent. The activities of this group do not make sense. Their attacks do not follow any real pattern and they don't have any clear motives, in fact it would make more sense if they attacked Fae villages. So I had them followed and watched, I followed the coin and it gave me a most surprising answer. An answer of who is actually deciding what villages are attacked." His casual tone carries an edge that makes my skin prickle. "And what an interesting answer it is."

He opens the folio, removing several documents. "Letters. Between the rebel leaders and someone in this very castle. Someone who provided detailed information about granary locations, guard rotations, trade routes." His eyes fix on Rowan. "Someone who wanted to create just enough chaos to turn the kingdom against its king."

The blood drains from Rowan's face. "You dare accuse—" he shouts, staring daggers at Milori.

"I dare present evidence." Milori holds up the papers. "Your seal, your signature. Quite detailed plans for destabilizing the kingdom. Though I must say, your handwriting could use some work." The smirk on his face isn't happy but rather one of grim justification. I can't stop my mouth from popping open at this news. He has been working to destabilize the kingdom?

King Leofric motions to one of his guards to bring him the papers. As he reads the evidence of his son's treachery, his face falls. Rowan bursts out—

"These are lies!" He lunges forward, but guards block his path. "Fabrications by the Day Court!" The room starts to murmur with excitement.

"Are they?" Milori turns to address the nobles directly. "The rebel attacks began shortly after the king announced Princess Alette's betrothal. Each one precisely targeted to erode faith in the crown. And who benefits most from a kingdom losing faith in its king?" His words hang heavy in the air. "The crown prince who would replace him."

Gasps ripple through the crowd as understanding dawns. Father sinks back into his throne, the weight of betrayal clear on his face as he stares at his heir—his favourite son.

"You would sacrifice your own people?" Duke Moonvale's voice shakes with fury. "Let them starve and burn just to gain power?" His questions hit the king and crown prince as if they were blades to cut them.

"The Fae are lying!" Rowan's composure cracks. "They want to turn us against each other! We can't trust—"

"We found your messenger." Milori's words stop Rowan cold. "The one you sent to meet the rebels last night. He was quite... informative, once we explained the consequences of treason."

I watch my brother's face contort with rage and fear. The perfectly controlled mask he's worn all these years finally shatters, revealing the monster beneath. The monster I know all too well. All those years of his cruelty, his careful manipulation—it was all leading to this. To him sacrificing innocent people in his grab for power.

"Father, you can't believe this." Rowan turns his attention on him, the look that he has shouts that he is caught but Father's shock has worn off.

"Guards!" Father's voice cracks like a whip. "Seize him!"

The guards move toward Rowan but he's faster than anyone expects. Steel flashes in the afternoon light as he draws a concealed blade from his sleeve. My heart lurches as he lunges toward Father, murder blazing in his eyes.

"If I can't have the crown, neither will you!" The words tear from his throat, raw with a madness I've never heard before. All his careful control, his years of calculated cruelty, dissolve into pure rage.

Everything happens so fast. The nobles scramble back, their shouts of alarm echoing off the stone walls.

Guards rush forward but they're too far away. Rowan is close to striking, Father half-rises from his throne, but age has slowed his reactions—he won't move in time.

Then the warm presence behind me leaves and I see Garrick move like lightning.

His massive form crosses the space between us and Father in two powerful strides. He catches Rowan's blade arm just as it descends, the force of his grip making my brother cry out in pain. The dagger clatters to the marble floor as Garrick twists Rowan's arm behind his back.

"Not today, little prince." Garrick's voice carries a dangerous edge, but he doesn't hurt Rowan beyond restraining him. Even now, even after everything, he shows more mercy than my brother deserves.

The guards finally reach them, taking hold of Rowan as Garrick steps back. My heart pounds wildly in my chest as I realize what just happened—Garrick saved Father. The man who imprisoned him, who would have executed him, and now owes him his life.

I race over to Garrick and he wraps me in his arms while we watch as they subdue Rowan.

He thrashes against the guards' hold, all pretense of nobility stripped away. "You're all blind! The kingdom needs strength—real strength! Not this doddering old fool who lets his daughter consort with monsters!" His insult should hurt but it only makes me proud that my so-called 'monster' is a better man than he or my father ever will be.

"The only monster here is you." Cedric's quiet words carry across the stunned silence of the nobility and the rustling of Rowan's struggle. He approaches Rowan slowly, disappointment and grief etched in his features. "How many died for your ambition, brother? How many children will go hungry because you burned their food?"

"Spare me your sanctimonious drivel." Rowan spits at Cedric's feet. "You're as weak as she is—"

His words cut off in a grunt as Cedric cuffs him hard across the face. Father still hasn't moved from his throne, his face ashen as he stares at his heir, his favourite son, now revealed as a traitor.

"Take him to the dungeons." Father's voice sounds old, tired. "Post triple guards. If he so much as breathes without permission, kill him."

As they drag Rowan away, his accusations echo off the walls. "You'll see! I'm the only one strong enough to rule! The only one willing to do what must be done!"

The throne room falls into an uneasy silence. Garrick leads me closer to Timas and Emilia, bringing me further away from the king of Windsmere. The bond between us hums its song as I relish his close comfort.

How can this be my life?

Father's eyes follow the movement, lingering on Garrick's arm around me. For once, there's no disgust in his gaze—only exhaustion and something that might be resignation.

"Your Majesty." Duke Moonvale steps forward, his weathered face grave. "The kingdom bleeds. The people suffer. What is to be done?"

The question hangs heavy in the air. Father looks around the room—at the assembled nobles demanding answers, at Cedric standing tall despite his grief, at me and Garrick joined together despite everything that should keep us apart.

"We will discuss the kingdom's future." Father's voice strengthens slightly. "But first..." His eyes meet mine. "Perhaps we should revisit the matter of betrothals and soul bonds."

Hope flutters in my chest, but I've learned not to trust hope too quickly in this place. Still, as Garrick's arm tightens around mine, I let myself believe that maybe there might be change after all.

Chapter 23

Garrick

The throne room is full of tension, the reality of Rowan's betrayal affecting the entire court. Milori comes up beside us once our small group is no longer the focus.

"I think the Human court is more entertaining than the Day Court. You need to step up your game in unforeseen revelations, Timas." Milori crosses his arms as he watches more arguing start up.

"This is not the type of antics our court needs. But if you want to be the court jester all you have to do is ask," Timas quips and I huff out a laugh, though I try not to do it too loudly.

"I think you've missed your calling, the court jester would be a better fit than the captain of the guard." My commentary may not be useful but it's the break in tension we need, and with Timas' smile, I have no doubt he might make him do it.

"Oh and you would do a better job than I, at being the king's captain?" Milori scoffs. "Unlikely."

"Are you really having this type of discussion right now?" Emilia chastises us but she is trying to hide a laugh in her whispered criticism.

"Is this a normal conversation?" Alette asks Emilia and she rolls her eyes so hard I wonder if they will fall out of her head.

"Yes. They are a bunch of children," she mutters. We laugh, but that anxious part of me is happy they're both happy and safe.

The king sits slumped on his throne, looking older than he did mere hours ago. Hard to blame him—finding out your heir orchestrated attacks on your own people would age anyone. Though watching him struggle with the betrayal does bring me a bit of joy. Does that make me a nice person? No, but he raised Rowan to be the calculating deceitful man he became and because of that I feel no sympathy for him.

"Your Majesty." Duke Wilmsburg's voice cuts through the noise. "We must address the immediate concerns: the people need reassurance, and the noble houses demand change."

The king waves a weary hand. "What would you have me do?"

"First," a new noble steps forward, one I do not know. He is younger than Wilmsburg and Moonvale but it appears he has seen a lot of war, as well as a bit seasoned in life. "It would be best to acknowledge the debt owed to the one who saved your life." His shrewd eyes fix on me. "The very one you wanted to execute not that long ago."

I resist the urge to shift under his critical gaze. These Human politics make my skin crawl, but I'll endure it for Alette.

"Yes." The king's voice carries a hint of... something. Not quite gratitude, but no longer filled with hatred. "It seems I owe you my life, Garrick of the Day Court."

The formal address catches me off guard. It's the first time he's used my name instead of 'Orc' or 'creature'. Whatever he may say next, I just hope it won't cause any trouble for Alette.

"I did what anyone would do." The words come out gruffer than I intended them too. Alette leans into me, a silent gesture of support.

"No." The king's face twists with something like pain. "Not anyone. My own son..." He trails off, unable to finish.

Timas steps forward, power humming subtly around him. "Perhaps this is an opportunity, Your Majesty, to right several wrongs at once."

The king's eyes narrow slightly. "Meaning?"

"A life debt is no small thing." Timas' voice carries that deadly calm that would scare any normal or sane person. "One that could be satisfied by releasing certain... claims."

Understanding dawns on the nobles' faces. The king looks between Alette and I, his jaw working as he processes Timas' implied meaning.

"The betrothal contract—" he starts, but Cedric cuts him off.

"Is void, by your own laws, Father." His tone allows for no argument. "Lord Bertram's actions saw to that. Unless you mean to argue that attempted assault is acceptable behaviour from a noble house?" Cedric stands with a strength and presence that befits an actual king and even his father sees this.

The gathered nobles murmur in agreement.

"The evidence of soul bonds cannot be ignored either," Cedric adds. "We may not have these bonds, but we have heard—even if only a rumour—that they are sacred, not to be trifled with. Considering the current issues at hand, would it not be best to save the kingdom from this particular case."

I should probably be offended that the vague idea of me going crazy is still being used to win this argument but if that is what it takes to get Alette away from this place then they can call me anything they want. So long as she is free.

The king's fingers drum against his throne. "Fine, Garrick is released and can return to the Day Court, a life debt clearing his crimes." He tries to straighten, attempting to gain some semblance of authority, though it falls flat.

"The noble houses have lost faith in the crown." One of the nobles shouts, the dissent in the group evident.

"The king can't be trusted." Another shouts.

The guards point their weapons at the unrest nobles and the tension in the room rises.

"I am your king!" he declares, but the authority he once possessed seems to be absent now.

"Perhaps there is another solution!" Cedric shouts over the growing voices. His voice commands attention and everyone quiets.

"What possible solution?" the king says through clenched teeth.

"A council, to share the burden of rule. To prevent any one person from wielding too much power," Duke Moonvale suggests and I can see the shock on the king's face. They want to strip him of executive authority. Well... this just got interesting.

"You mean to take my crown?" The king's voice carries more weariness than anger.

"No, Father." Cedric steps forward. He's proven himself a true ally through all this. "They mean to save it. The people need stability, now more than ever. A council, led by those who understand the needs of the people..."

"Led by you, you mean?" The King's eyes narrow at his youngest son but Cedric doesn't flinch at his harsh gaze.

"Led by someone who hasn't forgotten what duty really means," Duke Wilmsburg says in a sharp tone and it makes several nobles flinch. "Someone who stood against his own brother to protect the innocent."

I watch the king's face as he realizes he has no choice. His heir is a traitor, his kingdom teeters on the edge of rebellion, and the noble houses—most of them—stand united against him. Sometimes the best move is knowing when to yield.

"Very well." He sounds ancient now, defeated. "The betrothal is dissolved. The council will be formed." His eyes find mine. "And you, Garrick of the Day Court, are pardoned of all charges. A life debt must be paid."

Relief floods through me, but I keep my face carefully neutral. These Humans and their need for formal declarations.

"Thank you, Father." Alette's voice carries clear across the throne room. She doesn't move from my side, her quiet strength a beacon in this storm of politics.

The king looks at her—really looks at her, maybe for the first time. "You truly choose this?" There's something almost vulnerable in his question.

"I do." She lifts her chin. "I choose him, and the life I want to live. Not the one chosen for me."

He nods once. "Then go with my blessing, though I doubt you were going to ask for it." No, she wasn't, because my little ember is a crackling flame all her own now, a fire that has chosen me..

The nobles break into discussion about planning how this new council will work, Cedric already at the head of the formation. I have no use for their politics so I tune them out, focusing instead on the woman beside me. My soul bond, finally and truly mine.

I navigate Alette and I out of the throne room, away from all this. What I would give for quiet instead of these Humans chattering.

"Well," Milori appears at my shoulder, making me jump slightly. I really need to put a bell on him. "That went better than expected. Though I was looking forward to more dramatic revelations. Maybe even some furniture throwing?"

"Sorry to disappoint," I let out a faint grunt. "Though you could have warned me about Rowan." I glare at him, genuinely annoyed he didn't say anything.

He shrugs with that easy demeanor that earns him a brotherly punch. "Didn't want to ruin the surprise. Besides, you handled

it beautifully. Very heroic, very dramatic. The nobles ate it up."
He laughs.

"Is that all you think about?" I try to remain stern, but I'm fighting a smile now. "The dramatic effect?"

"Sure, why not? It would be boring if we went into these things well planned and informed." He scoffs. "Besides, someone has to think about these things. You certainly won't, Orcy-boy." I punch him in the shoulder as we navigate the halls.

"Hey!" He acts hurt but he is just looking for sympathy from people around him and lucky for me no one around him pays attention.

Alette laughs beside me—casting a sound of pure joy—and something in my chest finally unknots completely. We're free. After everything—the fighting, the fear, the darkness of denying the bond—we're finally free to just be.

"Come on." I take her hand. "Let's get packed and head back to Sonas." But then I realize we never really talked about this. About where we would go.

"Pft, way to assume." Milori and the rest carry on past us as I slow to a stop turning to fully face Alette. Her smile is so big it nearly breaks me. How is she so amazing?

"I'm sorry, I never asked where you wanted to go. Where would you like to go, my little ember? I will follow you anywhere." It's true I would follow her to the ends of the realm so long as I could be with her every day.

"I just want to be with you, Garrick, and with the family I have grown to love." She looks at Timas, Emilia, and Milori as they talk and laugh while walking down the hall.

"They are very difficult people, I can't promise they won't get on your nerves."

She laughs and it wraps around me. "I'm okay with that. But um..." She looks down, a blush creeping up on her cheeks.

"What, my little ember?" I softly trace her cheek, loving how cute she looks all flustered.

"What happens now, with us?"

I feel like a fool, again. "If you are truly convinced that being with me is a good idea—and I am seriously questioning your judgment—," She laughs again and I smile. "I would like to officially make you my soul bond."

"How does that work?" She chews on her lower lip, obviously nervous.

"Well it involves a lot of loud drums, a trip to an Orc temple, and you committing to this Orc who still can't believe you would want anything to do with him." I lean my head down onto hers and take a deep breath in. I want to be overwhelmed by her.

"I want that," she whispers and I can't stop the deep need to have her against me, so I pull her in tight.

"Then I will make it happen soon."

She laughs at me and puts her hands on my face, pulls me down to her. With the softness I don't deserve, she kisses me.

This world is full of hatred and pain but with her, it all melts away. I have my soul bond forever.

Chapter 24

Garrick

It has been a long couple of weeks to get to this point. Arranging to have our bonding ceremony in the Southern Clan territory of Dorrono took more time than I wanted, but we are here and it's finally happening.

The rhythmic beating of drums echoes through the mountains, their deep resonance stirring something primal in my blood. Smoke from the ceremonial fires carries the scent of burning herbs—sage and mountain thistle—sacred plants that have blessed Orc unions for generations.

I stand before the ancient stone altar, my formal attire a blend of traditional Orc leather and Day Court silk. Emilia was very annoying about having some Day Court symbol in the bonding ceremony. As if my little sister doesn't have enough power, she has to have an opinion about this. Absurd if you ask me, since she was raised as an Orc, but then Alette looked at me with those beautiful eyes and said it would look nice. As soon as the words 'honour your sister' left her lips...I was done for. But I guess it doesn't matter, so long as at the end of the day I am with Alette.

"Stop fidgeting." Father's gruff voice carries amusement as he adjusts my ceremonial sash. "You look like a nervous pup."

"I am nervous." The admission comes easier than it would have months ago. Controlling every emotion is an Orc's specialty. It turns out, something I failed to learn from my father, is that using emotion does not make you weak but rather strong because emotions invite criticism and only those strong enough can stand for it. "What if—"

"None of that." He clasps my shoulder, his scarred face softening. "The goddess chose well for you, son. That girl has more strength than half the warriors I've known." Pride floods my body at my father's praise. She is braver than most warriors because she fought against those who have been tying her down for years.

"Besides," Father continues with a rare grin, "Emilia would never forgive me if I let you mess this up. She's been helping Alette plan this ceremony for weeks and don't get me started on what Estola would do to me if I let you make a fool of yourself. I think she is tougher than I am, and I'm a seven-foot-tall Orc." Father laughs but he's not wrong. Estola might be a proper and distinguished Fae council member but she even frightens me.

"I gained her attention once when I suggested we have Orc ale for dinner and her stare was so cold I thought I froze," I mutter, because she truly is a terrifying woman. Father laughs and we both look over to Estola who stands with our clansmen like a statue of granite, holding her own among the wall of warriors around her.

Movement at the temple entrance draws my attention. Milori walks in, looking far too pleased with himself in his ceremonial captain's uniform. He takes his place near Timas, and for a split second, I question why he was even invited.

"What were you doing?" I holler at him as he adjusts his clothes.

"Nothing! Emilia just asked me to grab something, which I did because my queen asked me to." He looks at me annoyed like I did something wrong. Timas huffs a noise as if to say 'you better.' "Then, I got to see your bride," he casually drops and immediately I want to kill him. "I must say, she looks far too good for you. Maybe we should find her someone more suitable—perhaps someone devastatingly handsome with excellent hair..."

"I suppose that Orc who helped us unload our luggage would be suitable. He had nice hair." Cedric adds.

I growl at both of them, and in unison they just smile. "Touch my soul bond and I'll shorten that precious hair while you sleep."

"Can your big, chubby hands even hold shears?" he questions.

"Who says I was going to use shears? I can pull your hair out with my bare hands."

He stares at me for a moment before looking at Timas. "Do not get me involved. Besides, if you two fight before this ceremony begins, Emilia is going to have both of your heads and I will not stop *my* spirit bond." Timas adjusts the ends of his sleeves, as if merely annoyed by a fly and not threatening to unleash his wife on us.

"It's an Orc ceremony, they would be happy for a fight, even Emilia knows that," my father comments and I smirk at the slight shock on Timas' face.

"I do not get your customs," Timas mutters.

The shift in the drum beat pulls my attention back to the entrance of the tent where Emilia comes walking in with her blue formal gown that matches Timas. These Fae and their matching clothing. She slides in beside Timas before raising an eyebrow at us. "If you two are done with whatever this is," she gestures between us, "we have a ceremony to begin."

"Told you," Timas mumbles and Emilia turns her ire on him which makes Milori laugh.

My heart pounds as I take my place before the altar. The gathered crowd—a mix of Orcs from my father's clan and Fae nobles from the Day Court—creates an odd audience but somehow represents our family well. What's most surprising is that so many from the Day Court showed up here in the mountains but I guess I shouldn't be surprised any more.

Another shift of the drums and she appears.

Alette walks toward me in traditional Orc ceremonial dress, but somehow she's made it entirely her own. The deep green leather is adorned with silver symbols of both our cultures. Her hair falls in waves around her shoulders, woven with small braids in the Orc style. But it's her eyes that capture me—those hazel depths that first called to my soul, shine with a joy that takes my breath away.

The bond surges between us, stronger than ever. No more fighting it, no more running. This is where we were always meant to be.

"My little ember," I whisper as she reaches me. She takes my hands, and the rest of the world falls away.

The ancient priestess steps forward, her face marked with the sacred tattoos of our ancestors. In her hands, she carries the soul-binding cord—woven from leather strips dyed with mountain berries and strengthened with the prayers of a hundred unions before us.

"Life of the mountains," she begins in the old tongue, her voice carrying the weight of generations, "heart of the storm." She wraps the cord around our joined hands, each loop accompanied by the deep beat of drums.

"As the mountains endure, so shall your bond endure," she continues, switching to the common tongue so all can understand. "As the storm rages true, so shall your hearts beat true." The cord tightens with each word, a physical manifestation of the bond we already share.

The priestess takes a small bowl carved from ancient mountain stone, filled with sacred spring water blessed by the morning's first light. She dips her fingers in the crystalline liquid and traces the ancient symbols of unity on our joined palms. The water feels cool against my skin, but where it touches, a warmth spreads through me like forge-fire. As the blessed drops fall onto the sacred cord binding our hands, the drums reach a fever pitch.

I barely register the words, too lost in Alette's eyes. The way she looks at me—like I'm everything she's ever wanted—it still feels like I'm dreaming. The bond pulses between us, stronger than ever as the priestess continues the ancient rites.

"The goddess has joined these souls," the priestess' voice rises above the drums. "Let no power in this realm or sky, in mountain or valley, tear asunder what she has bound. What the goddess has blessed, let all here witness and honour."

As I lean down to kiss my soul bond—my wife—the drums reach a crescendo. The bond flares golden between us, visible for just a moment. The elders say it is a blessing to see the bond and show it to those gathered around us.

After a gentle kiss I pick her up and throw her over my shoulder. She squeaks at the sudden movement but the room erupts in howls and grunts from the Orcs while many of the Fae startle at the sudden noise. I shout my joy from the top of my lungs, proud to have my soul bond complete.

—----------------------------------

The outside of the temple is set up for a celebration meant for an Orc. Though it is mixed with some Fae elements. The Fae wine they brought is flowing and many of my clansmen are drinking it happily, a strange sight to see if I am being honest.

Looking around I see those who are my true family. Emilia and Father laugh as they share an Orc dance of sharp movements and stomping feet.   Timas actually smiles while he talks with Estola and Milori. Well, Milori *is* being his usual self, only this time he's talking with an Orc woman. I wonder if *my brother* realizes she is showing her interest in him... I'm sure it'll be fine. Emilia brings Alette out to Father and shows her how to dance, her smile so bright I'm smiling. My family...

Emilia heads towards me but I keep my eye on Alette and Father.

"I told you it would work out." She bumps my arm with her shoulder as Alette twists under Father's arm, her laugh carrying across the gathering.

"Yes. Yes, you're very wise." I pull her into a one-armed hug. "Thank you, Em. For everything."

"That's what family does." She squeezes me back. "Just next time will you please listen to me first. I'm really smart." I look down at her, so proud to call her my sister. But, I don't let that stop what I really want to do. I grab her tight and start rubbing her head, messing up her hair like I have done since we were children.

"Garrick, you great oaf! Stop it!" I laugh as I let her go and she glares at me. "If it wasn't your bonding ceremony I would have Timas do something to you but because I am a nice sister I am going to tell you to go get your bride." She huffs out but I don't wait. I do exactly as she says and go towards my bride.

Somehow Milori has taken over dancing with Alette while I was speaking with Emilia. Milori dramatically dips Alette while she laughs. I shake my head, but my heart is too full for any real annoyance.

"Time to find someone else, Milori. This one is mine." I step in and swiftly take Alette's hand so she twirls into me instead, her laugh a joyous melody.

"Ah well, I knew it was only a matter of time." He smiles. "I guess I should find a new partner or some more of that Orc ale, better than the stuff you had at the palace." He laughs.

"You could always go back to that woman you were talking to, she was giving you the customary sign that she would be interested in taking you as her partner." I wag my eyebrows and his face drops, making me almost double over in laughter.

"What! You're kidding..." He looks over at her and she is still watching him with her tusks protruding more at her smile. "Maybe I shouldn't drink any more ale... I'm going to go find Timas, he'll make sure nothing happens to me." He backs up slowly, terrified now by the attention he has garnered and that makes this day even better.

"You're so mean to him," Alette says as I spin her around and back into my arms.

"He deserves it; it's what family does."

Her smile is bright and her eyes glitter in the candle light. "Family. I like being a part of this family." The earnestness in her voice threatens to break my heart. She has lived for so long without any real family. Even Cedric, who is now on the other side of Father talking and laughing, hadn't acted like her brother in years.

"You're my everything, Little Ember. And we will have the life you always dreamed of, I promise." Her eyes mist at my words and I gently rub her cheek.

"I love you, Garrick."

"I love you, Alette, from today until the end of our lives where even still our souls will be bound. You are my everything." While leaning in to kiss her, the people melt away and it's just her and I forever.

Chapter 25

Alette

Several months later

The manor of my broken childhood looms in the distance, but I don't feel anger or resentment towards the place... just a simple apathy instead. Returning to this place feels different now. With Garrick by my side I feel like it is just another piece of myself I want to show him.

The iron gates that once felt like a prison bring to mind memories of trying to climb them with Cedric and laughing as we both fail.

"You're sure about this?" Garrick's large hand engulfs mine as we slow to a stop in front of the manor. The building is simple, yet extravagant—especially compared to the homes surrounding it. The two story building with large arched windows and flowers that engulf the exterior speak of wealth and influence. Fascinating how something this elegant can look like a home to one and a prison to another.

"Yes." I squeeze his fingers. "Cedric says she's doing much better. The new physicians he arranged have helped immensely.

Besides, it's been several months since our bonding ceremony and I think it's time you met her in person." The warmth of his hand wraps around me and I unashamedly take comfort from his presence.

"Alright, whatever you want, my little ember." His lips brush against my hair, sending shivers of affection across my skin. His gentle caresses still leave me breathless and I'm not sure I'll ever get used to it.

He climbs out of the carriage, putting his hand out so I can easily exit. My lovely purple Fae gown flows down to the ground, the sun catching on the threads to make it shine. Never again will I wear those restrictive dresses Father forced me to wear. Garrick doesn't care what I wear so long as I am comfortable. He even said Orc women wear pants with loose tunics and he would have been happy to find me those if I wanted but I like these dresses, they make me feel beautiful.

The stone steps leading up to the main door are perfectly clean, no dirt in sight, a fake presentation I do not miss. The butler—Bartholomew, but I have always called him Bart—opens the door with a warm smile on his face.

"Miss Alette, it is so good to see you." His warm voice brings tears to my eyes. He was always a safe person within the manor–a person I could count on. Without thinking, I walk quickly over to him and wrap him in a hug. With gentle hands he hugs me back, delicately patting my head like he has done since I was a child. "It's good to see you too sweet Alette." I try not to completely come undone but some tears fall anyways. Pulling back, I look into his kind, brown eyes.

"I've missed you." I muster all the sincerity I can because I truly have missed his stable and warm presence. He was always there when Mother was lost in her own thoughts.

"I missed you too. No one to keep out of trouble since you departed."

I laugh and it sounds a bit watery but it's nice to see him. He squeezes my shoulders and looks at the very large man behind me; Garrick. He doesn't act surprised or show any form of disgust. He bows his head slightly to honour Garrick and it warms my heart.

"Wonderful to meet you—" He pauses for a moment, stuck on what to call him.

"Garrick, just Garrick." My soul bond responds, the easy way he responds to Bart makes me melt inside.

"Of course, Garrick. I am happy Miss Alette has found someone so willing to protect her." His words threaten to open the flood gates but miraculously I manage to keep it in check.

"Just Garrick. Don't let this nice jacket fool you. I would prefer to be in much more casual attire but I wish to make a good impression on Alette's mother." Garrick steps closer to me, pulling me into his side. My absolute favourite place to be.

"I am sure she will adore you so long as you make Alette happy. Though it was a very enjoyable experience to watch her find out you are an Orc. I don't think I have laughed so hard in years. I was afraid her face was going to be stuck in the stunned position for years but she warmed to the idea quickly when Master Cedric told her what you did for Alette."

My heart feels like it is going to burst with the collision of my past and present. Garrick wipes away a tear but I just smile.

"Now, don't do that, Little Ember. You know how much it hurts to see you cry."

"I'm just happy. Happy you finally get to meet Mother and Bart."

Bart smiles, that warmth I depended on for years exuding from him. "Come, your mother is waiting for you in the gardens. She is rather proud of herself. She planted a new section and it looks wonderful. Oh, but pretend I didn't tell you that. She wants to share that with you." He shakes his head at his loose tongue and leads us inside, through to the garden.

We find Mother sitting on an elegant garden chair drinking tea and smiling–actually smiling. Since moving to Sonas I have only communicated with her through letters. Cedric tried to teach her how to use the Fae communication orbs but he said that just confused her and that she preferred writing the letters. I could tell she was getting better every month, the letters were longer and more detailed. She would even share things she was excited about. We have been planning this trip for a while but after what happened at Windsmere, when Garrick was pardoned, the Human kingdom has been tumultuous. So we waited, as per Cedric's instructions, until things settled down a bit.

She looks up as we approach, and my breath catches. There's awareness in her eyes that I haven't seen since I was small. The usual fog that clouded her gaze has lifted somewhat and her smile is genuine, not forced.

"Alette." Her voice is soft but present. "And this must be your Garrick." The way she says it, like she's been waiting to meet him, makes my heart squeeze. All of this would not have been possible mere months ago. I am so grateful Cedric found good physicians to help her.

"Mother." I step forward, uncertain how to navigate this new version of her. "You're looking well."

"The gardens help." She gestures to the flowers around her. "They always have. I'd forgotten that for a while." There's pain in her admission, but also clarity. "Come, sit with me. Tell me about your life in Sonas."

Garrick helps me settle onto one of the chairs beside her, then drifts away to 'look' at the flowers to give mother and I some time. Mother takes my hand and looks at me, really looks at me.

"I'd forgotten how beautiful your eyes are," she whispers and I choke down a sob.

"Oh, Mother." I try to pull in my emotions but I struggle and several tears come pouring down my cheeks.

"I am so sorry, my precious daughter. You deserved so much more." She seems to wallow around in her own emotions. We sit together trying to regain some composure but, for the first time since I was a child, I see my mother. Before me sits a visage of the same woman who used to spend evenings reading to me.

"Your garden looks lovely, Mother," I say after finally finding my voice. She smiles and gazes upon the section of flowers before her.

"Thank you, my darling. These were gifts from the Fae king and queen. Very nice of them to send flowers from Sonas. A truly kind gesture. I thought it would be best if I planted them since they were a gift."

I'm surprised. I didn't realize they sent my mother flowers. She touches one of the petals while I turn to Garrick who is still near enough to hear what is going on.

"Emilia insisted your mother have something beautiful to look at. You're family, Little Ember, and so is your mother." Garrick softens his voice so as not to scare Mother. I expected her to ignore us, but instead she laughs and I am struck speechless.

"Little Ember?" Her eyes sparkle with interest. "What a lovely name." She turns back to her flowers and my eyes fill with tears. I feel like my entire world has shifted by seeing mother doing so well. Garrick just smiles.

Before I can respond, footsteps approach from the manor. A moment later, Cedric walks into the garden with a smile on his face. "I thought I heard voices." He beams with happiness and I stand to hug him when he gets close.

"Cedric." Mother's voice carries genuine warmth. "You didn't tell me they were coming." I knew he wanted to keep it a secret, just in case something prevented us from coming.

"I wanted it to be a surprise." He takes the other chair and sits with us. Something in my chest eases at how peaceful and right this feels. "Besides, I knew you'd just worry about having everything perfect." He side-eyes her but he's smiling and so is she.

"As any mother should," Mother teases and I can't believe what I am seeing. Smiles, teasing, joy. It is filling my heart with so much joy. Cedric's frequent visits and the new physicians he arranged have worked wonders.

"Even with the council keeping you busy, you're still able to visit?" I ask my brother and he smiles warmly at our mother.

"Every week without fail." Mother's hand finds Cedric's, squeezing gently. "He brings books and reads to me. Just like you used to."

Tears prick my eyes at the memory—of sitting in this very garden, reading stories while she stared into nothing. But now she's here, present, asking about our lives and actually hearing the answers.

"I spent too much time away. I have communicated with the council that this is important to me and will not be negotiated on." Cedric has grown so much in the last several months. No longer is he the quiet boy who did whatever Father and Rowan said. Now he is a man who stands for his values and fights those who challenge them. I am so proud of him.

"Now, tell me more about Sonas," Mother requests. "Are you happy there?"

I look up at Garrick who has come closer, likely feeling the ease of the situation. When our eyes meet he closes the distance so he can touch my shoulder in a gentle and caring way. His blue eyes still captivate me and his love has become a comfort I never knew I was missing.

"Very happy, Mother. I've found where I belong." I smile turning back to her.

"Good." She touches my cheek gently. "That's all I ever wanted for you, even when I couldn't say it." Her honesty brings so much peace to my heart. Her awareness heals a part of me that always wanted to see her get better.

The morning passes peacefully as we talk. Mother asks about Emilia and the Day Court, actually laughing at stories about Milori's antics. She listens intently as Cedric describes his work with the council, pride shining in her eyes.

When Garrick finally relaxes enough to sit with us, he shares tales of his forge and the magical weapons he creates, and she shows a genuine interest. She even reaches out to touch his arm once, thanking him for making me happy.

"I am tired now. I must rest, but I look forward to your stay with me, my darling." She smiles as she stands, wavering slightly on her feet. Cedric stands as well to steady her.

"I am happy I came and I am so happy you are doing so well, Mother." Her smile warms me as she places a gentle kiss on my cheek, finally giving me the motherly affection I'd craved throughout my childhood years.

Cedric walks Mother to the front of the garden where Bart stands waiting. Garrick comes closer as if sensing how overwhelming all of this is for me.

"She's truly happy," I utter.

"She has someone who is able to care for her here–someone who can fight for her. You did everything you could back then, Little Ember." His words strike my heart and heal it all at once. I always wished I could have done more, but there was nothing I could have done. I lean into him, finding that strength he often gives me and relishing it.

Cedric comes back and takes his seat again. I can see the circles under his eyes and the stress in his face. He was hiding it from Mother.

"Things are not going so well at Windsmere?" I inquire as I sit up to really look at Cedric.

He pushes out a breath and looks out at the garden, the exhaustion becoming much more apparent.

"Father has not been an easy man to deal with. Even with the council in place, he still tries to make deals and negotiates contracts to try and get more power back. It has become a large part of my responsibility to find out what he is up to." He looks back at me with a smile. "But the kingdom as a whole is getting better. Much of the tension between the noble houses has settled except for the very strong few in the south. Rowan is also a high maintenance prisoner." He rakes his hand through his hair. "But these are not things you need to think of. Tell me how everyone is in Sonas?"

His genuine care for my new family brings me so much joy.

"Things are tense at the moment. There have been more attacks on some of the outlying Fae villages. Timas has had to send out whole teams to root out the rebels on the different islands but there always seem to be more popping up."

"We're not sure how it's even possible, there shouldn't be that many rebels," Garrick grumbles. "Our attack in the shrouded forest eliminated all of the staunch supporters of the old king. Milori has been using every possible contact he has in trying to discover their true intentions." His voice grows annoyed. We may not have a lot to do with the politics going on in Sonas but, with being related to the queen, we are often informed of what is happening.

"It's a shame, really," Cedric says, but there is something in his voice that says there is more and Garrick catches it too.

"Do you know something?" Garrick doesn't hesitate to question, he is not a man who is going to wait around for answers either.

"Part of the reason I wanted to be here when you arrived is because we have heard some rumours. I have a network of people who gather information for me and just recently we have heard a rumour that the Fae rebel group is close to finding the artifact."

Garrick and I look at each other confused. Artifact?

"What are you talking about Cedric?" I ask him.

"That's just it, we really don't know much more than that. Several people on the coast are getting reports of smaller groups of Fae crossing the ocean in the middle of the night. Some have heard these people talk about an artifact that was lost a millennia ago. It doesn't make sense to me or those collecting the information but I assumed Timas might know what it might mean. Or Milori." Cedric takes a sip of his tea while Garrick and I run through this new information.

"Have you heard Milori talk about this, Garrick?"

Garrick and Milori have gone on several trips to help some of the villages that were attacked but I don't recall him mentioning this.

"No. This is news to me." He shifts in his chair as if he is ready to go find out exactly what this means.

"We should tell Milori," I suggest before a look of discomfort crosses his face.

"Milori went back to his island to visit his mother. Apparently, she is sick. There is a concern that she may not survive her illness."

I turn to look more fully at my husband. "What!? Why didn't I know about this?" I'm hurt he didn't tell me.

He takes my hand and rubs it gently. "I knew you were nervous about this trip and I didn't want to add to your stress. He told me just as we were leaving–but–he wasn't sure the information was true. He was going to send me a message when he knew for sure, so I was waiting." I understand why he did it but I don't like it.

"Fine, but next time you tell me," I demand and he smirks at my stubborn stance. I am finding it a lot easier to ask for what I want now, which seems to make him really happy. I send a quick smile at him.

"Of course, Little Ember." His lips meet mine in a swift, gentle kiss, and I feel warmth rush to my cheeks at his tender gesture. "I'm going to send a message to him now. Are you fine if I leave you for a moment?"

"Of course." I smile at him as he gets up and heads to where our luggage is. We have an orb with us just in case we need it.

"It's good to see you so happy, Lettie." I look over at Cedric. The weariness is still there but he does seem happy.

"I am happy. I didn't realize that finding someone to love would bring so much joy."

He smiles at me. "Maybe one day we will all receive such a gift, though I guess a soul bond is out of the question for me." He laughs, but I see the longing there.

"I don't think an Orc would be a good fit for you, Cedric, but I know there is a woman out there just waiting for you to find her." He laughs and we talk about what she might look like or where she might live.

We face a future of so many unknowns, but one thing I have learned is that with those you love surrounding you, you can face even the toughest of problems. My family may be a mix of all the races of this realm but I wouldn't trade them for anything.

Also by TM Goodkey

If you enjoyed this story would you please consider reviewing it on Amazon or Goodreads? Any Review is greatly appreciated! Thank you for considering it!

<u>The Elemental Dominions</u>

Strong Mental Health Rep and a Slow-Burn within an Epic World! Try out this series.

Sowing Deceit: Book 1

<u>The Qadia Realm</u>

H is Hidden Heart

oving the Kraken

Acknowledgements

This story was a bit of a whirlwind. I may have put myself on a tight deadline BUT that only means I finished it right on time because lets be real I would have procrastinated hard anyways.

Thanks to my family who suffered through me writing like crazy and thank you all for reading the continuing story within the first world I somehow imagined!

Stay tuned for Milori.

Love from Ontario!

TM

About the author

Making dwarves blush, orcs believe in love, and elves lose their cool - that's what TM Goodkey does best. Living in Ontario, Canada, she's beyond happily married with two beautiful children and a backyard full of chickens (which, according to her kids, definitely count as pets). An avid reader of ALL things magical/fantasy with a side of romance, TM has been a published Indie Author since May of 2024. She writes closed door romantasy filled with funny characters, swoony moments, and everything in between.

You can find her here:
Website- www.tmgoodkey.com
Facebook- TM Goodkey Author
Instagram @tmgoodkey